NAKED SUN

ROBIN BALOGH COX

KNOWHERE MEDIA

Disclaimer

The characters and events portrayed in this book are fictitious. Any similarity to real persons, living or dead, is coincidental and not intended by the author.
This book is intended for entertainment purposes only.

The author and publisher, Knowhere Media LLC, shall have neither liability nor responsibility to any person or entity with respect to any loss or damage caused, or alleged to have been caused, directly or indirectly, by the information contained in this book.

I would like to dedicate this book to my son Layton Jacob Cox who inspired, in name only, not in character, the wild west villan within and in loving memory of Steve Gandy whose life stories inspired and entertained and without whom Tucker Montgomery's character would never have been born.

1

—————

"Come on Bev, you know you could use a break."

Tara had no idea how true that was.

Bev laughed into the phone. She hadn't had a day off since she took over as editor in chief of the Alpine Avalanche newspaper six months ago. Getting her bearings in the new position coupled with the complications of the physical and emotional recovery from her near death encounter with the previous editor, not to mention the several months she had devoted to the failed reunion with her ex-husband, had been a whirlwind.

A break was well deserved.

When the town council of Alpine asked her to fill the empty editor position Bev had jumped at the chance to have complete journalistic control of the hometown newspaper, not fully understanding what that entailed. She had definitely glamorized the idea in her mind.

She couldn't deny the sense of justice, satisfaction, or perhaps karma, she felt at the offer. After all, Hal Preston had tried to kill her...twice. It seemed only fitting she should have his newspaper. Little could she have known the job itself would be her un-doing.

"I just don't know how I can get away Tar. Who will run this literary empire?" Her sarcasm wasn't lost on Tara.

Tara continued to press, "It's only for four days! Four glorious days of lounging poolside, drink in one hand, book in another. Tucson is perfect this time of year, tons of sun. The resort is all inclusive and it's on me." Finally, she paused, waiting for Bev to answer.

Bev sighed. It did sound tempting.

"It would have to be from Thursday to Sunday, and I would need to do some work."

Tara sensed Bev's defenses falling. "Not a problem, the resort has WIFI! Is that a yes?"

Bev was sure Tara was already packing. "Okay, yes."

"Great! We're going to have so much fun!"

Bev heard the silly college girl tone in Tara's voice. The same tone she had grown to love during their shared University of Colorado days, and a little something more mischievous. Tara definitely knew how to have fun.

"I'll pick you up Thursday, early. I'll call. Gotta go! " Tara was off the line as quick as she came, leaving Bev with a list of questions on the tip of her tongue.

"What time?" she asked no one on the phone.

"What should I bring to wear?" she continued to herself.

"Fantastic!" She put the phone down and went to inform her staff of her plans.

Elena was at her post manning the grey metal desk in the reception area. She hadn't missed a beat when Bev had taken over the paper. She hadn't seemed surprised in the least when her previous boss had turned out to be a killer either and seemed to have no more or less regard for her current employer.

Bev had since decided that Elena's allegiance was first to herself, then her family, then Her Lady of Guadalupe, then perhaps her job. She was, however, a great receptionist–when she was there–and Bev needed her general knowledge of the systems at the paper. Elena, of course, knew this.

"Elena?" Bev approached her as a jester does the queen.

Elena looked up through long black lashes. She had the kind of beauty that Bev was sure was sung about in the Spanish ballads that played on the radio behind her. Songs that spoke of "mi Bonita", "mi Vida", "mi Corazon", "mi Amor". Intimidating to say the least.

"Elena," Bev tried again. "I am going out of town Thursday and Friday." Elena didn't react. "Will you send Ramon to me when he comes in, we have to move the paper run up a couple of hours?"

The Tejano crooner sang on, "no mas", "te quierras".

"I also need to get last week's run sheets and advertisers list."

Elena acknowledged and turned, moving to the files behind her. In moments she handed the requested files to Bev.

"Thanks."

Bev headed back to her desk. There was a lot to do in order to leave. She usually investigated the police reports on Tuesday, but she would have to move that up. She would call Lela at the police station in a few minutes.

She paused. The police reports always made her pause.

She hadn't seen Sam in eight months. That in itself was amazing, given that they both worked in a town with two stop lights. She dreaded the day they would see each other. Thankfully it hadn't happened yet. She didn't know what she was going to say to him if and when it did. Instead she waited for the weekly police reports, pretending not to care, and then spent the rest of the week trying to forget him all over again.

She knew it was passive stalking, verging on becoming an obsession. She knew it, but she looked for his name listed in the paperwork anyway. She knew he had been promoted. He was Sergeant Samuel Gant now. She knew he was on a special team, it wasn't clear what their assignments were, maybe narcotics. There were several drug busts attributed to the team, which would also explain the lack of his presence in town. He definitely wasn't on traffic patrol anymore. Lastly she knew that he had a new partner and she went only by the nick name "B". Perhaps for security purposes.

In an act of sheer cowardice and vague hope she had left any absolution of their relationship up to him and he had stayed away. Though she had first met him a little over a year ago, it seemed like ten since he had pulled her over for speeding on the way to get a job at this newspaper.

He had been a chauvinistic, arrogant, macho cop. She had been the idealistic, nosey, journalist. Gasoline and fire that had combusted into an explosive affair. They could never catch a break. There had been her ex, a murderer, and several trips to the hospital. And finally there had been her fear. Fear of failing in another relationship. Fear that he couldn't help her overcome.

She knew they were over, she just didn't have time to process all of it fully. She also knew she really didn't want to, so she pushed the thoughts aside once more and went about her business.

Bev made the necessary calls to the police station and met with Ramon. There were two articles she needed to finish and her letter from the editor to write. Classified Ads would need to finish their copy early and she would have to come up with the lead story and get the front page photo. Elena reluctantly fulfilled Bev's request to contact the schools to get their lunch lists for the upcoming week and the Honor Roll List.

There was never enough time in a day. By 9:00 that night Bev's list was considerably shorter, but far from finished. She flipped the lights off, the last to leave the building, and she would be the first to flip them back on in the morning. Such was a day in the life of Editor in Chief of the Alpine Avalanche.

She sighed. Suddenly Bev felt tired and realized she was very much looking forward to the weekend getaway with Tara.

2

———

Father Miguel took a deep purposed breath. He loved the smell of the church, the beeswax that coated the thick stucco walls, the lemon oil on the mesquite wood benches, the fine desert dust mixed with the scent of burned sage incense and candle wax. The smell was clean and cathartic.

He loved the heavy silence in the cool air of the pre-dawn desert. He could hear his heart, he could hear his thoughts, and he could hear his God. He loved his God and he loved where God had placed him to serve.

Mission de Santa Catalina in the Ciudad Mia Nuevo was a 200 year old Franciscan mission church that had become the center of the prospering southwestern town. It had been established to minister to the local Pima Indians in the late 1600's by Jesuit priests from Spain. Over time the church had succeeded in converting the indigenous tribes, helping them turn from their pagan worship and tribal warfare to the passive cultivation of the rich river valley which inevitably brought prosperity and civility to the region.

The church stood at the heart of the traditional town

square, an anchor and center piece to every town activity and every life event of its parishioners. Baptisms, weddings, funerals, Saint's feast, Holy holidays, weekly mass and daily confessions made it a solace and a symbol of God's faithfulness. The whitewashed tower and belfry literally pointing the way to heaven.

There was a school for the children, an infirmary for the sick, a monastery for the called and an orphanage for the fatherless. God's work was being done. Father Miguel was certain of that. However, recently there were things that concerned him. There was an uneasiness in his spirit. He sensed dark motives amidst the joy of his congregants. He took another deep breath and prayed for clearer thoughts and a clearer path.

He was kneeling at the foot of the altar, eyes closed, the only perceptible movement in his body were his hands, expertly rolling the rosary beads through his fingertips, and the slow easy rise and fall of his chest. The first rays of morning light cast benevolent golden beams of sun across his back and the wooden floor beside him. He reached the end of the prayer row and waited, calming his mind. God's peace could only be found by a calm mind.

"Dear Lord," he whispered. "Give me the wisdom to know Your will and the strength to do Your bidding. I pray for Your Holy Church and for its followers. Give them Your peace and direction, Your healing in their spirits and bodies. Show me opportunities to serve You and reflect You to them in that service. Protect us God my Father.....In the name of the Father, the Son and the Holy Spirit." He kissed the rosary and crossed himself

The morning bell rang with the dawn of another day in the Lord's house, a worthy crescendo to his fervent entreaty. That bell, that beautiful bell, the only one of its kind in the territory, maybe in all the world. Cast well before Father Miguel's time, it was a rare beauty in this harsh land. A bell plated in pure silver, made for a pure God, to call the faithful to purity.

The Jesuit priests who had led the way in this desert and started this mission had cast the divine instrument. Soon after their arrival they learned from their new local converts that the surrounding desert mountains contained gold and silver. A great deal of gold and silver. It wasn't long after that Spain knew as well.

After the Jesuits explained their eternal debt of the tribes to "the one true God", and the debt of gratitude they owed to Mother Spain, the Indians could think of no better way to pay their homage. The ore was gladly mined and donated by the Indians for the benefit of God and Spain. The priest's too, at first, considered the mine a divine appointment and worked side-by-side with their native brothers.

Over time, however, the work became grueling. The mountain trial was treacherous. And as it often had before, man's tenacity for the heavenly waned under the strain of worldly toil. Several Indians and priests lost their lives bearing their loads. The Indians, still new to Christianity, became afraid and began to combine their superstitious pagan beliefs with their newly learned doctrine. In order to appease their lesser gods, a sacrifice would have to be made in hopes of warding off future disasters.

They planned a ceremony in which the tribal chief's son would be married to the kidnapped daughter of a warring neighboring tribe and then she would be sacrificed. Her blood would cover any sin that had been committed by removing the precious metals.

The princess was captured and raped but before her

blood could be shed, the priests learned of the ceremony and interrupted the sacrifice. The Indians were beat into submission, imprisoned and starved until they were convinced that the only way to repent of their pagan ways was to continue their mining work. What had started as a partnership quickly deteriorated into a slave-master relationship.

The priests enslaved the Indians to mine the precious metals, using the gold and silver to ornament their mission and please their monarchy. Greed infiltrated the church and the minds and hearts of the priests like a putrid disease. After some time the Indians lost all faith in their cause, and this new found god, and were determined to end their suffering.

Using the guise of a large new find of silver ore, they easily lured the infected priests, sick with the lust of this world, into an ambush. They killed their captors and the Pima people left the "cured" holy men and piles of their treasure in the mine, closing it forever with a solid silver door.

The Indians then free, disappeared into the illusory desert landscape of the Catalina Mountains along with any and all knowledge of the mine. It was never discovered again, although many sought to find it.

If that was all it was, a legend, an ugly blot on the history of the mission, Father Miguel's heart would be at peace. After all, God's will had many paths and just as many converts had been made in times of strife in the church's history, maybe more, as in times of peace. The very reason he served at this mission was because the Franciscan brothers he belonged to replaced those very priests that fell to the Indians.

God's will always finds a way.

But there were rumors, whispers, a recent unrest that could only be born of greed and ungodly selfish pursuits. Gold had been discovered again in the Catalina Mountains, the legends of the lost mine was resurrecting, the sickness was returning.

Men's hearts were so easily turned by the powers of this world, so easily infected. Father Miguel feared for his parishioners. He could sense a fever rising in the village. He didn't know what the changes would mean to his village or his church, but he knew change was coming.

He lifted his gaze to the sculptured face of the Crucified Christ above the altar. He looked into his Savior's eyes, finding immediate comfort there. This Christ who took away all sin, all sickness. Father Miguel didn't know, but his God did, and Father Miguel trusted his God.

He crossed himself and rose from the floor. This mission had stood for nearly 200 years and by God's will it would stand for 200 more. He would trust his God.

YESIDRO DESANTIAGO MADE his way down the steep narrow path of the desert mountain using his one good eye. His burro, also visionless in one eye, followed faithfully behind him, one tiny sure footed hoof in front of the other. Y, as people called him, had always joked that God had made he and the burro two halves of a whole since they were blind in opposite eyes.

They were making their way slowly into the valley to the town of Mia Nuevo, hoping to quench the unrelenting thirst that only comes from weeks and months in the desert. A thirst for the sound of a human voice, for fresh water and food, and for liquor from a bottle, not from a cactus.

"He sees the left half and I see the right. The half in the middle wasn't meant to be seen," Y would chuckle through his missing teeth and wandering tongue, widening his white cataract eye for effect. As if on cue his burro would curl back his lips as if laughing at the tired joke.

No one was certain how old Y and his burro were, yet everyone knew him. It was suspected that he was well over one hundred. Generation after generation told of Y and his one eyed companion coming and going from the mountain. Time had not changed them. On the contrary, decades in the desert had somehow preserved them.

Sometimes if enough free tequila was offered in the saloon, Y 's one good eye would glisten and he would tell wild stories of years ago. Stories of wild native Indians, kidnapped Indian princesses, human sacrifice and of a silver mine that only he and his one eyed burro had ever seen.

"I had two eye's then, saw all of it. I know the way," he would spout assuredly.

If the lucky patron who inadvertently sat next to him at the bar was a stranger, he would just nod politely as Y continued his rant. The locals would nod politely and pay for another shot of his tequila.

It was on one of these nights, during one of his rants, that a stranger offered Y another drink and sat down beside him.

"I have been listening to you old man." The stranger sat with his back to the bar, elbows bracing his weight. "Your stories interest me." He turned to look at Y, keeping his gaze fixed on the one good eye.

The stare stopped the old man. He tipped his dusty, sweat soaked hat back on his head and tried to focus on the man in front of him

"Oh they do, do they.." He rubbed his silver stubble chin, a jack o lantern grin spreading across his weathered face. "Which ones?" He lifted the empty shot glass towards the stranger who understood and in turn summoned the bar keep to fill the glass again.

"The one about the mine," he said casually as he watched Y throw back the shot and lick the last drop out of the bottom.

"Ohhhh...they all like that one. Lots of takers on that one." Y blinked slowly. Finally he mustered, "What's your name?"

"Don Santos Juaquin," the stranger offered.

"Saint Juaquin, huh? The father of Mary, if I got my 'caddy cism' right..."

The stranger nodded and smiled at the old man.

"Yes, he is my patron saint. Honored of God." He poured another drink and passed the glass to Y. "Will you tell me old man? Tell me about the Lost Silver Mine."

Y paused, his caution had dissolved with the tequila.

"Sure, Santo Honored of God! Sit back, this one will cause your hair to curl, or maybe cause you to lose an eye." Y snorted, slapped his new friend on the shoulder and began to tell his tale once more.

3

———

*B*eep–beep–beep!

Tara's horn repeatedly pierced the crisp morning mountain air.

Bev was madly throwing things into a bag. She had said early, but 6:30am was not a leisurely way to start a vacation weekend in Bev's mind.

Beeeeeep! Beep!

Bev was sure the neighbors would call the cops. She had moved into a cute stucco duplex tucked up against the base of Sleeping Lion mountain in Fort Davis, just across the street from the century old Presbyterian Church. As a rule it was very quiet, apart from the church bells on Sundays, until this morning. Tara was going to wake the living, the dead and the lion in the mountain with her racket.

Bev bounded out the door with a half closed suitcase in tow, waving with her one free hand in hopes of silencing the beeping. Tara's red hot convertible Corvette was visually as brash as its horn, but suited Tara perfectly.

"Could you be any louder?" Bev grinned at her friend as she stuffed her things behind the seat and climbed in.

Tara hit the horn again for effect. "I honestly don't know how you stand this sleepy little town."

They were moving before Bev could settle in her seat, dust flying behind them. If the neighbors weren't awake before, they were now.

Tara was grinning like a Cheshire cat behind big sunglasses as they swung out onto the main road. Bev grinned, too. Finally someone else to take the wheel. Despite the wild ride, she donned her shades and settled back into the contour leather seat. This was going to be fun.

The air moved relentlessly, making it difficult to catch her breath. The constant hot breath of an unseen monster blew from one direction, then the opposite. Bev could never get a fix on its location. She knew it was sinister without ever seeing its form. It taunted and twisted her like a bug caught in a web. The helplessness and impotence she felt against her attacker was terrifying.

A tiny spark of light flashed and lit the pitch darkness. It flickered and moved with the air. Bev twisted and searched in the dim illumination, but there was still no sign of her adversary. The spark grew quickly into a consuming blaze. She struggled to leave, but couldn't.

No. Not again! she thought. With a jolt Bev jerked awake and cried out, grabbing the dashboard in front of her instinctively.

"Sorry, didn't see the pot hole. You okay?" Tara looked over the top of her sunglasses questioningly.

"Man," Bev physically crumpled back into her seat in relief. The dream had been reoccurring occasionally since the fire. She narrated some for her friend.

"Wow, creepy. I'm sure it's just post traumatic symptoms. The fire had to be terrifying and your unconscious is just now letting go of some of the fear." Tara sounded confident.

"Sounds reasonable."

Bev wasn't sure that was the whole explanation, but who was she to argue. She had always had poignant dreams of past, current and future events. Something she had really never divulged to her roomy. For now she was just glad to be awake.

"Where are we?" Bev unfolded the map at her feet. She had never been this far west before and although the scenery wasn't much different from the desert southwest of Texas, there was a difference in the air.

"There's only one road to Tucson, I-10. Can't miss it. Need to stop? You were asleep for a while." Tara wasn't waiting for an answer, she slowed down for the next exit.

"Sure, let's eat." In her rush to leave Bev hadn't had anything that morning.

The day was turning hot and the air conditioner struggled in the corner of the gas station diner, making sure sounds of an electric appliance dying. They stuck to the vinyl booth seats and drank luke warm ice tea from sweaty glasses. Bev loved watching people. She studied the clientele.

The diner had obviously not changed in many, many, many years. Chrome edged the worn Formica topped tables, the bar and the padded bar stools. There was a tired family of four in the back booth. Past the point of exhaustion, the parents were letting the children play with the condiments. The staff looked equally as enthused to be there as the paying customers. A waitress attended the pies on the counter in a glass case that turned automatically, if not jauntily, around and around. A man sat next to the case.

He was very thin, weather worn clothing and face, not very old, probably homeless and hitching. He watched the pies temptingly swing by then lurch out of view. The waitress behind the counter asked if he wanted a piece. He shook his head and pointed to the coffee cup in front of him on the counter. She filled it up and he went back to watching the pie.

Her social study was interrupted by their own waitress. She and Tara ordered and as the waitress turned to leave, Bev caught her arm.

"Would you put a piece of pie on my ticket for that gentleman at the counter as well?" The waitress named 'Jen', according to her name tag, raised an eyebrow. "Our secret." Bev smiled at her.

Tara shook her head. "You bleeding heart," she jibbed. "Always making me look bad."

They laughed. Out of the corner of her eye Bev saw Jen offer the pie and the man looked around the room suspiciously, then he shrugged and chose his slice.

"So...I have a surprise about our little trip!" Tara exclaimed.

A sudden sense of dread came over Bev, erasing the euphoria of her good deed.

"Oh no...what?" She leveled her gaze at her friend. If you could call her that.

"This is not an *ordinary* resort," Tara teased, raising one eyebrow suggestively.

"What do you mean *not ordinary*? It's not a singles place is it? Because you may as well just turn around and take me home. Have you forgotten the last time we went to one of those?" Bev was trying to keep her cool.

"No, no...not a singles place. And actually I thought we had a great time the last time." Tara smiled wistfully, recalling the event.

"You mean you had a great time. If you remember right both nights we were there you left with both men we were talking to! I sat and listened to really bad karaoke." Bev was starting to panic.

"Ohhh to be young again," Tara laughed.

Bev had visions of the piles of work on her desk and four days wasted.

"Seriously Tara, where are you kidnapping me to?" Bev growled.

"Don't be so dramatic. It's going to be a blast..." she paused for effect. "We are going to one of the premier clothing optional resorts in the nation!" Tara clapped happily and bounced in her seat. It took a minute for the words to compute.

"By *clothing optional* you mean.....?!"

"Nude," Tara whispered lustily.

"Nude!" Bev's voice rung out. The man at the counter turned with a forkful of his pie, the whole restaurant stopped. She lowered her voice to a hiss. "I am not going to a nude resort." Bev grasped the edge of the table as if to secure herself from being bodily taken away.

"Don't be such a prude, you'll love being nude. Ha! That rhymes!"

Tara took Bev's wrists and flattened her hands on the table top between them as if to steady her.

"You have to admit...you're curious," Tara tempted.

Somehow this silly woman knew how to goad her. There was a moment of silence. Tara continued to pat Bev's hands and grin impishly.

"Seriously? Nude?!" Bev finally retorted.

"Ha! I knew you would do it!" Tara threw up her hands and clapped again.

"You waited until we were almost there so I couldn't back out didn't you?" Bev was kicking herself for not asking enough questions and demanding the answers.

"You betcha," Tara laughed again.

Jen brought their food and Bev sulkily picked while Tara dug in.

"I don't know how you manage to con me into these things." Bev shook a limp French fry at her.

"Oh my God! You would not have a life at all if it wasn't for me, and you know it." Tara shook one of her limp fries back.

She was right. Much more than half of the adventures in her life had been spent with Tara.

Bev took a deep breath, "Fine."

They ate in silence for a few moments. Tara also knew when not to gloat.

"Finished?" Tara asked. "We want to get there before dark. Don't want to miss any of the sights," she snickered.

Bev followed the bouncing blonde out the door to what she was sure was her doom or, at best, another weekend of pure personal humiliation.

4

Two well fashioned bankers sat on one side of an ornate walnut table in an equally well fashioned ornate office. The deep wood tones and faded scent of expensive tobacco further eluded to the wealth in the room. They faced four men, equal in tenacity, if not in fashion, ready to make a deal.

"You're willing to bear all the risk? No compensation if the money is stolen or lost? No guarantee?" William Fargo leaned forward placing his hands flat on the table.

John Butterfield grinned and leaned into the banker. He was no stranger to risk. A wealthy man in his own right, he had struck many risky deals before this one. Some of them had paid off, some had not. Unlike the bankers in front of him John Butterfield wasn't addicted to the appointments of wealth, but to the risks involved in acquiring it.

"I have my guarantee." He tipped his head indicating Tuc Montgomery and Jake Layton, whose large dusty frames sat uncomfortably stuffed in the red leather chairs beside him.

"Very well," Henry Wells stood and reached for Butterfield's hand. The rest of the men stood on cue and the deal was struck. "We'll have the papers sent to the hotel. Livery will be ready at the end of the week. What about the stage?"

All eyes turned to Scott Willson, the fourth man in the party. He smiled. As the driver he was in charge of livery and carriage.

"The coach is ready when you are. She's fast and sure," he stated.

"Good. We will meet once more to discuss the final route," Fargo paused. "If you get through we'll make history boys. History...and a lot of money."

The thought made them all smile as the company departed. When the oak door closed, Henry Wells walked to the walnut credenza and poured himself and Fargo a whiskey from a cut crystal decanter. He handed his partner the drink.

"Can they do it?"

They stood shoulder to shoulder at the window watching the four men that had just left their office make their way down the main street.

Fargo took a drink before answering, "I've bought some insurance. If they can't, no one can."

***

Y woke, as he had every day for the last ten years, surprised to still be alive. It was like being born over again each morning, ripped from the deep dark warmth of slumber into the cold harsh bright light of day. Every one of his senses was acutely aware of some offense.

His head and body ached, his eyes burned, his ears rung and his mouth was dry and spit-less as dirt. Keeping his eyes closed, he took a deep breath just to be sure he still could.

The coughing that ensued racked his withered frame forcing him to acknowledge that he was indeed still a sojourner on this earth. His second deep breath was a sigh of resignation.

Today, however, when Y finally opened his eyes, his surroundings surprised him. He wasn't in the church ward or the backroom of the bar as usual. He was in a bright white stucco room. There was a silver cross on the wall and a high set window that let the light in and the heat out. It was not hot despite the time of daylight, the room was pleasantly cool. The bed he rested on was comfortable and clean and he had a woven blanket over him. He lay still, breathing the cool air in and out, not wanting the few comforts to end. Perhaps he was dead. If so he wouldn't mind.

When Y was younger he had never anticipated being this old. The act of living had become tiresome, difficult and painful. Y had just decided to close his eyes and tempt a final rest again, when there was a knock at the door.

"Señor DeSantiago?" a woman's voice inquired.

Still might be heaven, thought Y. After all he was only old on the outside, his heart and his desires were still young.

"Si?" he responded curiously. He had not been called by his proper name is a very long time.

"Quieres un poco de comida?" she asked through the door.

Food. That was a thought.

"Si! Entrar."

The old man raised up and slowly swung his legs off the side of the bed. A slight Indian woman came in with a tray and set it beside him. Never making eye contact.

"Pardonde, Señora." She stopped, he continued, "Donde estoy?"

"La casa de Don Juaquin." She closed the door behind her leaving him to his meal.

The last evening's events began to take shape in his mind. He had met a man at the bar. They had been drinking, or more likely, *he* had been drinking. He ate as he pondered. The tortilla was warm, the coffee black, his head continued to clear. The man, Juaquin, had asked about the lost mine, wanted to hear his story.

"Interesting," thought Y out loud. His burro heard his voice and brayed from a yard not far away. He and the burro safe and sound at Don Juaquin's.

Y hollered back, "Very interesting." And finished his meal.

5

———

Bev had seen plenty in her life. She was no prude and had never been ashamed of her own body. However, she couldn't keep her jaw from dropping as she and Tara registered at the resort lobby.

Everything was just as it should be, the historic stucco and beam building, the hand hewn well worn stone front desk and the turn of the century western art that adorned the room. Only the middle aged woman behind the desk jumped blindingly out of the setting.

She was approximately as wide as she was tall, grey curly hair on her head bounced to the rhythm of the rest of her flesh as she busied herself with the paperwork– completely in the buff. Tara chit chatted with her as if there was nothing unusual.

"All of the public spaces, like the pool, the club house and the tennis courts are nude. The restaurant and the trails are clothing optional." The desk clerk pointed to a map as she explained. Tara nodded and smiled.

Bev was still absorbing the situation when a very tall thin man with a wide brimmed straw hat, and nothing else, strode through the lobby. Her eyes were drawn to his obvious nudity and she was glad she was still wearing her sunglasses. He smiled and went out into the gardens beyond.

Note to self, thought Bev, *wear sunglasses all weekend.*

"Here's your key. You're in the historic wing. It used to be the old stage stop." She handed them a flyer explaining the hotel history along with their key, all smiles.

"Thanks!" Tara said a little too enthusiastically. "I know we'll have a great time."

Bev followed Tara out through the lobby, pretending to be attentive to her rolling suitcase. They passed through a small bar where three older men sat bare assed and bellied up to their beer watching a sporting event on the TV above.

Wow. Naked bartender, too.

Thankfully, they had no further frontal exposures as they made their way through the traditionally desert land-scaped gardens to their room.

"Cactus and nudity? Do you think that's a wise combination?" Bev asked as they passed into the small but well appointed stucco room.

"Don't be such a Debbie downer," Tara scolded. "We have way too much luggage," she chuckled, throwing her suitcase on the corner stand.

"I'd say." Bev stashed hers, too. "Are we really going to do everything nude?"

"Why not?" Tara was already disrobing. "Everyone else is. Think of it as another one of your social studies of human nature, ah natural." She threw her underclothes on the bed and donned a sarong around her hips, her sun hat and glasses. "Ready," she laughed.

Bev took a deep breath and did the same, grabbing her book as she left. She could hide behind the cover and pretend to read if she had to. Subconsciously, she straightened her shoulders and sucked in her stomach as they traipsed off to the pool.

———

THE SLAMMING pool gate announced their arrival. Bev was sure every eye was upon them as they set themselves on two lounge chairs in the corner of the fenced area. When she took off her sarong and no one applauded or booed, her heart rate finally began to calm.

She was very glad for her glasses as she perused the 'nude' zone, careful not to stare too long. It was an interesting mix of people. She would never have guessed that most of the body types represented would delve into this particular hobby. Her perception of perfectly tanned and toned bodies was quickly abandoned. There were tall, short, fit, fat, light, dark, adorned, inked, old and not so old. What amazing variety and not a one of them perfect.

More power to them, she thought as she watched a very large couple bobbing around the pool together.

There seemed to be three types of naturalist, as the info card had described them. Those that hung out (no pun intended) on the fringe of the activity, laying in the sun or reading like well schooled lizards. Those that were extremely active, playing water sports, walking to and from the bar and visiting with others. And those that were somewhere in between, comfortable in their own skin but not parading it around.

Tara lounged casually, making sure she had sunscreen on her most delicate parts. Watching the activities behind large dark glassed and the rim of a floppy hat.

"How did you come up with this?" Bev asked as she

continued to watch male and female of the species parade by.

"A friend of mine came with her husband. They had a great time. She basically dared me to try it." She dismissed the whole thing with the wave of her hand indicating it was a stupid dare. "I haven't noticed any deviant behavior. Everyone is actually more polite than when they're clothed. I knew you would get a kick out of the human nature of the naturalist. This is not a swingers or lifestyle resort. They have those, but I thought this sounded more appropriate for us. Want me to get us a drink?" Tara boldly stood, no sarong, to walk to the lobby bar. She waited for Bev's order.

"Sure." Any inhibitions she had would be toned down with booze. "Get me a white wine."

"Check." Tara moved gracefully around the pool to the lobby door and disappeared.

What an odd thing. All this nudity and no hanky panky. Bev wondered how wild the lifestyle places got.

There was almost an innocence about it. An equalizing. Most places she and Tara had been the women were scantily clad or topless, but the men's most vulnerable parts were always covered. She liked the fairness of this place, maybe it was her journalist nature.

Feeling more comfortable she relaxed back, closing her eyes. The sun and the air felt energizing and natural. She actually liked the sensation. It was difficult to tell where her skin ended and the air began, like they were melting together in the heat of the naked sun.

She was just dozing off when she felt a spray of cold water.

"Cute, Tara. Just give me the drink," she said with eyes still closed and hand out.

"Sorry," a definitely male voice responded.

Bev jumped in such a way that in hind sight (no pun intended) she was sure certain body parts jiggled unflatteringly.

"Oh! No, I thought you were my friend." Bev scrambled to sit upright, at least cross her legs. The gentleman in front of her was older, but fit and tan, everywhere, greying at the temples and not unattractive.

"When you're naked, everyone is your friend." He smiled and held out his hand never losing eye contact. "Hi, I'm Steve."

Bev shook his hand.

"Beverly, or Bev, to my friends." She smiled back. He had the most amazing dark blue eyes.

"Nice to meet you. Do you come here often?" He sat on the lounge chair next to her and continued drying off.

"No," Bev chuckled. "First time. I would have thought the complexion would give that away."

"Not necessarily. Some nudists like shade."

"So have you been a nudist long?" She wanted to keep the conversation going. He was the first man she had spoken with, other than Ramon the pressman, in a month.

"About ten years. I stopped coming for a while when my wife got sick but decided to come back to it a year and a half ago after she passed away." Steve looked down for a moment. "It's addictive."

"I'm sorry about your wife." Bev made a quick judgment and didn't discern a pick up, just genuine conversation.

"Thanks. How about a happier subject? What do you do for a living, Bev?" Now he was keeping the conversation going.

"I'm the editor in chief for a small town newspaper in Southwest Texas." Bev scanned the lobby door for Tara, she could really use that drink. She was sitting buck naked with a buck naked eligible male, but without any liquid courage.

"Wow!" Steve was genuinely impressed.

"It's not as big a deal as it seems. A lot more to do with printing machine mechanics than actual journalism."

Tara walked up behind Steve and cocked her head. A "well, well, well" look on her face.

Steve turned.

"Hello," Tara offered. "I'm Tara."

"Steve." He stood as both women watched. "I've taken your chaise."

"No, no. No worries. I can pull up another one." Tara handed off the drinks to Bev and started to find another chair.

"No, it's no problem. I'm just heading out to do some hiking before sunset. I'll leave you two to your sun worship." Steve turned to go, putting the damp towel around his neck.

"Nice to meet you," Bev said and meant it.

"You too! Always good to make a new friend." Steve smiled, put on his sun glasses and walked away.

"My, my, my," muttered Tara as both of them watched his very brown ass disappear.

"Unbelievable," said Bev taking several gulps of wine.

"Why is it unbelievable? You're quite attractive, laying here naked," Bev interrupted her.

"No I mean, I am, I mean we both are completely naked and I don't think we lost eye contact once. It was like we connected on another level." Bev took another drink.

"Ahhh. Well out of politeness you have to look people in the eye when they're naked, otherwise they would think you were a perv."

"Hmm," Bev thought about the protocol of nudism and

about Steve's ass and drank the rest of her wine. Tara watched her.

After a few moments, Tara exclaimed, "I knew you would love it!" She slapped Bev's thigh and they both laughed.

6

Willson held the eight reins gingerly in his palms, sensing the varying wrenches and tension from each animal. He was an expert driver day or night, at one with the coach and team.

Two narrow wagon ruts lay ahead of the team's pounding hooves. Sixteen strong legs pulled, clattered and stumbled on, moving the stage and its occupants into the night before them. When one began to tire he was pulled on by the endurance of the others, and they were all steadied by his hand on those reins.

The noise of beast and burden was deafening. The dust, suffocating. Wheels rang against rock, wood frame creaked, leather strained against binding, teeth ground and men groaned. Somehow by grace or luck the whole transport, men and horse stayed in one piece, lurching onward into the night.

Tuc Montgomerey tried to close his eyes and leaned his sore shoulder against Jake Layton's, trying to keep from being thrown from on top of the stage. Jake's chin was on his chest. He snored as his neck acted like a spring, absorbing the jolts from the ride.

"Amazing," Tuc muttered to himself.

The childhood friends had been through some rough times and close scrapes and no matter what, Jake had always been able to sleep. Indian camps where they were likely to be scalped, rocky ledges where they were likely to roll to their death, open desert where they were likely to be snake bitten, Mexican village whore houses where they were likely to get shot or rattling stages where they were likely to get pitched under knife edged wagon wheels...it didn't matter, Jake could saw logs.

Tucker, on the other hand, tended to worry. He thought about the dangers, anticipated the horror. He had seen too many men die and killed enough to know that their days were numbered in this rough unforgiving land. He was pretty sure that his keen sense and anxiety had kept them both alive longer than they deserved. It was his role on the team.

Jake's job? The fastest draw, the daring, death defying exhibitionist, the dreamer, the deepest sleeper. Jake snorted and rolled towards the edge. Tuc grabbed his jacket and pulled him back towards himself. He would follow his friend anywhere, do anything or kill anyone for him.

"Shit." Tuc tilted his head back and watched the stars above dance with the rhythm of the stage.

They were 12 days into the route. The job at hand wasn't particularly dangerous, other than the damage to internal organs from the shaking, and the pay was good. They were to keep the Wells Fargo bank box safe through transit. Hired guns to guard the strong box. If they succeeded they would be the first to make the 17 day trip and move the monies inter-continent. Tuc shifted his weight again, feeling the box beneath his back side. It made for a damned uncomfortable seat.

There had been rumors of robbers through the Arizona territory in the Catalina mountains, particularly in the stretch from Maricopa to Gila Bend. Local banditos thieving from scared women and dandy business men headed west. Not many of the previous stages had made the entire journey and none of them had held the wealth of this cargo. They wouldn't stand a chance against he and Layton. They had taken out ten times as many men in Texas fighting against Santa Ana.

He replayed the memory in his mind.

The sun had just begun to come up over the canyon rim where they sat waiting. They weren't entirely sure if they had been in Mexico or Texas. It didn't matter in this border war. If you came across the enemy you shot them.

They had discovered the camp the night before. Definitely Mexican nationals, probably making their way to meet the army that was amassing near San Antonio.

Jake had correctly estimated the amount of tequila that had been consumed the night before based on the lack of energy that was going into breaking camp. When Tuc had turned to Jake to ask what to do next, he was gone. A quick search found him down the canyon rim heading for the horses that were tied at the west end of the camp.

"Crap," Tuc had muttered as he pulled all of his guns from his holsters and lay them on the rock face in front of him. Three hand guns and two rifles. He would play sharp shooter and obviously Jake would be hand-to-hand. He steadied the first rifle, as soon as the horses were loosed there would be a scramble, like ants in a disturbed ant hill. Their initial count had been 20 to 24 men. He would have to reload quickly and rely on some well-oiled timing between he and Jake.

Jake moved quietly among the horses with very little reaction from the animals. Tuc watched the camp. One of the men stood up, scratched and moved to a nearby shrub to piss, never noticing the movements of Tuc's partner. Tuc set his site on him just in case. Jake waved when he noticed Tuc on the ledge at ready.

"Yeah, yeah..I see ya," Tuc replied out loud and signaled back.

Jake grinned, drew his gun and fired into the air, the shot ringing off the wall of the canyon like a bell. The horses bolted, Jake jumped behind a nearby boulder and, just as expected, the Mexicans scrambled and rolled from drunken stupors to the closest cover.

Tuc didn't waste any time. He shot three men before they could stand, changed guns and wounded two more. Jake shot from the opposite end through the dust cloud the horses had left in their wake. Three more men fell. A handful ran down the canyon after the horses. They wouldn't be back.

Jake and Tuc held their fire, saving their bullets for more worthy targets. Tuc could see three men huddled behind the piss bush. They appeared to be loading weapons. Tuc could also see a string of arms left fireside. Some of them were unarmed. Jake was still unseen and two men were heading towards his hiding place unknowing. Jake looked to Tuc. Tuc held up two fingers. Jake nodded.

As the men rounded the rock they were met with sudden and imminent death, two quick sure shots. The men at the other end of the camp fired blindly up the canyon toward the sound believing they were the targets. Tuc shot one of them in the head and Jake moved.

Tuc moved, too. There had to be four to six men he couldn't see right below him. He wanted to keep them guessing as to his position. Jake's gun rang out, ricocheting off the rock behind Tuc.

"Shit," Tuc knew it was a warning.

He turned and looked up from where he had come. Two men scrambled after him. He squared his large frame and shot both shot guns braced from his hips. The men flew backwards. If they weren't dead they would be soon. Tuc did a mental count, only two to four left.

Jake's gun shot again. This time below Tuc. He dropped the shotguns and drew his revolvers. Tuc Montgomery was 6'3" and near 300 lbs, stealth was not his strong suit, but he managed. He couldn't see Jake or the other two men that had been behind the shrub, but he knew how his partner fought. He would be constantly moving towards the opponent, a dangerous and unnerving tactic for everyone involved.

Tuc could hear the men below him, 15 feet away maybe. They were breathing hard from fear, adrenaline and maybe injury. They spoke in Spanish. Tuc could make out *'gringo... marshall...muerta'*. There were three speaking and one groaning and cursing.

A man yelled from across the camp, another shot rang out. Tuc knew without seeing that the men behind the shrub were dead. Jake was closing in.

The three below shot back at the sound, not knowing where or what to aim for. Tuc sat still, giving Jake time to make his way into position, more than likely he would come around from the southeast end. More urgent desperate Spanish from below *'municion, Dios, Santa Maria'*. The groaning man was silent. Three men left

Tuc stood silently, the butt of his guns felt solid in his

hands, familiar, his thumbs at ready to cock the hammers. He took deep even breaths. Then he heard it, a slight shuffle in the shrub to the southeast beyond the whispering men. Jake didn't wait for the men to hear him, he flushed through the mesquite like a startled bird, guns blaring.

Tuc moved around to flank him as the men fell into the dust. Jake turned grinning, but too soon. The injured man lifted his pistol aiming at the back of Jake's head. Tuc's hands moved habitually, cocking and firing his pistols in succession around Jake, killing the injured man instantly.

Jake slapped Tuc on the shoulder, never flinching or missing a step, grinning from ear to ear.

"Thanks, big T!"

"My pleasure."

Sitting atop the rattling stage coach, Tuc chuckled at the memory. He closed his eyes. "God save us both."

7

———

Bev woke to the soft breathing of Tara in the bed beside her. Hysterically they had both dressed for bed after a pleasant afternoon at the pool, a lovely dinner and a rousing round of karaoke, all without a stitch of clothing. Bev grinned again at the irony and decided to go find coffee.

She started out the door with her nightgown on, realizing she didn't need it as the neighboring elderly couple strolled by in their saggy baggy elephant skin in the all-in-all.

What a hoot! she thought to herself and tossed the nightgown back into the room. She strode towards the main office where she recalled seeing coffee service.

Sun poured like liquid light over Sombrero Peak spreading down the desert valley. The mountain was shaped exactly like the Mexican hat it was named for. The air was cool but not uncomfortable. The resort was relatively quiet.

Bev found her coffee and took some literature from the lobby about the national nudist society and the history of the resort, settling at an outdoor table in the sunny courtyard. She quickly lost interest in the Nudist Association magazine. Lots of naked people at board meetings.

The history of the resort, however, captivated her curiosity. Originally a ranch stage stop in the mid to late 1800's, the place had seen its fair share of gunfights, Native American and Mexican scuffles, as well as drought, famine and fire. Bev knew about fire, past a present. It was a constant treachery in the old west.

She shivered, a recall of her own recent escape from the lick of deadly flames. How hot was a fire in Arizona? She read on.

Wells Fargo stage company had made many of its first runs through this stage stop, unfortunately it had also been repeatedly robbed. Determined to stop the financial blood-letting of its stages, the company had hired gunmen to guard the cash cargo and escort it to its final destination in San Francisco.

During one of these guarded trips the stage had been robbed at this very stop. A gunfight had ensued. There was some confusion as to who had actually survived. The gunmen and the robbers were never accounted for and neither was the gold. Stories were told of the perfect heist and buried treasure actually on the property in the nearby hills. Bev's imagination ran wild.

"Wonder who took who?" Bev looked at the photo of the stage crew, scrutinizing the two hired guns. "Hmm," she said out loud to no one in particular.

"Puzzled?" asked a familiar voice.

Bev turned. Her new friend, Steve, was sitting at the next table with his back to her, reading the local paper. Of course, he was naked.

"Good morning," Bev greeted. She hadn't heard him being seated.

"Good morning," he grinned warmly looking over the top of his sunglasses.

"I was just reading the history of the resort," she offered. "I have a thing for historical stories."

"Brief me. I haven't read it yet." He put his paper down inquiringly.

She took a few moments and filled him in on the basics.

"There are all sorts of buried treasure stories in this part of Arizona. I'm not surprised that this place has one, too." He took a sip of his coffee. "They have a hike up to Sombrero peak from here that follows some of the gold trails, interested?" he asked casually.

"Hmmm. Hiking."

He sensed her hesitation. "It's clothing optional." He drew out the last word.

"Ha! You read my mind. Somehow, naked hiking, it gives a whole new meaning to fanny pack."

They both laughed.

"If we go, we have to start pretty soon. It gets warm even this time of year."

"Well, we can always take off our clothes." She winked at him, while at the same time thinking *I can't believe I said that!*

"Nothing lost, nothing gained," he retorted without skipping a beat.

"What time?"

"How about in an hour? Invite your friend, too."

"Right. Back here in an hour."

She had completely forgotten Tara in the interchange. She stood, and perhaps it was her imagination, but she thought she could feel him watching her as she walked away.

All's fair, she thought and went to rouse Tara, who by

nature, wasn't an early riser or a hiker. Bev thought it was fitting that she enjoy everything this weekend had to offer.

THE TRAIL WAS moderate to challenging in parts. Bev was glad that she had chosen a sports bra and bike shorts for the trek. Steve and Tara had quickly stripped down to get some sun while they hiked. Strangely it all seemed like second nature now. Bouncing body parts didn't even draw the eye.

They had passed from the grease wood scrub brush into an unbelievable saguaro forest. The limbs of the distinctive cactus pointed this way and that. They made charming replications of people dancing, bending, and gesturing. All naked and not caring. The desert was beautiful. There was really so much color when you took the time to look. Grey green, bright orange, flaming red. It was amazing.

The sun rose quickly, but they were also climbing in elevation and it wasn't too hot yet. The group decided to stop at an outcropping not too far ahead for a water break and a quick bite. The goal was to get to the top of Sombrero Peak before noon, keeping the easiest part of the walk, down hill, for the warmest part of the day. Each of them packed a gallon of water. The rule in desert hiking was, no matter what, when you have used half of your water you have to turn back. So far so good.

They reached their stop and spread their shed garments on the rocks as a thin shield against scrapes before resting against them. Bev joined in and stripped down. They chatted casually about the view while drinking their water and munching on power bars. Bev retold the story of her fall from the overhang in Fort Davis while trying to get a selfie, amazing them both. They all agreed that they should have a nude photo of their stop.

"Okay," Steve fumbled with the iPhone aiming it at the women. "Get closer together. My friends would never believe me if I told them what I was doing right now."

The women laughed and posed.

"Let's try to get all three of us," Tara gestured for Steve to join them.

"No ledges, right?" he toyed with Bev, tossing her the camera phone.

There was a sound. A thud.

It didn't register with Bev at first, but in less than a second she watched Steve, who had started to move towards them, slow and stop mid-stride like he had hit an invisible wall, then he fell backward. She turned to inquire from Tara what was going on. There was another thud and she watched her long time friend crumple to the ground. Instinct took over and she lunged for the ground herself.

Gunshots.

Her mind was spinning. Steve's tan feet were facing her, he wasn't moving. She glanced over her shoulder, Tara's beautiful body lay awkwardly in the course sand.

"Tara!" she whispered urgently. She moved closer to her, the gravel scraping her body. She had completely forgotten she was nude.

She turned Tara over. The front of her skull was gone, leaving a gaping hole above her beautiful blue eyes. They were wide open. She had been expertly shot from behind. Blood mixed with water from a tipped over water bottle beside her and was quickly absorbed into the thirsty ground.

"Oh my God...Tara," Bev whimpered hoarsely.

Her heart pounded, adrenaline coursing through her

veins. She suddenly felt very exposed and vulnerable but afraid to move. She was sure whoever shot Tara and Steve were still out there, still watching.

She forced herself to move on her stomach, passing Steve. One shot to the head, from the front. Death was instant. She tried not to let the bile and the tears choke her. She had to get on the other side of the rocks, away from where the shots had come from. She stopped for a moment, thinking she may have heard movement or a distant voice.

Nothing. She kept inching.

Finally reaching the rock, she took three quick breaths jumped to her feet and rounded the stone. She waited. No sound, no gun shot. She tried to breathe. Only after she took a full breath did the tears begin to stream down her face.

What horror movie was this? It couldn't be real. It was a ghastly nightmare, not the girl trip adventure. Maybe it was one of her dreams. That hope evaporated with the reality of the sight and smell of blood on her hands and belly. She was working herself into hysteria, shock was beginning to set in.

She squatted, panting like a caged animal huddled next to the large rock, trying not to lose it.

She shut her eyes tight and tried to take deep breaths to settle her mind and her senses.

Just as she had begun to focus, streaming her energy into her next move and her ultimate survival, a large hand grabbed her mouth from behind. She fought blindly, scratching, biting, kicking, knowing now that her only chance of survival was to unleash that animal she was trying to squelch.

A man. He was large and he wrapped around her with both arms before she could do much damage. She was too incensed to scream, instead she made guttural noises that she had never heard herself make before. His mouth was close to her ear and he was shushing her like a child as he pulled her off the outcrop and into the scrub brush desert.

She tried to bite his hand, finally succeeding. He didn't flinch as she drew blood, but continued pulling her further into the wild of the desert.

It took a little time, but suddenly she realized he was also watching, keeping eye for some unknown foe. For the gunman?

Something about his movements, calm and swift, the tone of his voice as he shushed her, none of it was that of an antagonist. She decided to relinquish and move with him. Then, in a sudden rush of understanding, she was certain he wasn't after her, she was certain he was saving her.

He literally carried her backwards through the brush still keeping one hand tightly around her face and the other arm around her middle. Her feet barely touched the ground. When they were about a hundred yards down the mountain from the outcrop, he stopped, breathing heavily through his nose.

"I'm going to let go of your mouth," he whispered in her ear. She nodded. "You cannot make a sound," he warned. "They are still out there." She nodded vigorously again.

Slowly he let his hand go and she breathed deeply and slowly. He still kept her tightly around her waist. He shook his loose hand, finally acknowledging the pain she had inflicted. She felt extremely light headed and nauseated. He bolstered her up, sensing her losing consciousness.

Hot tears poured down her cheeks, she bent at the waist and vomited. All the while he held her upright.

"Oh God!" she whispered when she stopped retching.

Something in his frame changed, he released his grip around her waist and turned her to him. Despite the warm

temperatures she was shaking uncontrollably, teeth chatter-
ing, blinded by tears.

She let him wrap her in a coat and he held her. She put
her head on his chest taking deep breaths. Oddly, it was all
too familiar. Then she knew. The sound of his voice, the
smell of his chest, the way he moved and held her. She
raised her head in disbelief.

"Sam?" she whispered.

He put his finger to his mouth, blood running down his
forearm from her bite, and pulled her back into his chest.
How she wanted to scream, to jump for joy, to slap him all at
the same time. Instead she just breathed in and out, trying
to absorb all of this.

"We have to keep moving. Are you all right?" For the first
time their eyes actually met. Those beautiful grey, telling
eyes. They were anxious, serious and alert. All she could do
was nod.

He tilted his head to keep going in the direction that
they had started. She nodded again. Pulling on his coat, she
went ahead.

"It will all be all right," he reassured her, placing his
hand on the center of her shoulder blades. She knew that he
was the only one that could convince her it would be.

8

———————

Scott Willson's long grey hair hung down the back of his worn leather duster in a single pony tail. It swung from side-to-side as he worked, mimicking the tails of the horses he attended.

He spoke in quiet tones, moving easily between the exhausted animals. They relaxed at his touch and in moments he had them expertly unharnessed and was leading them to the stage stop paddock. He checked the leathers, gathered the fresh horses and began re-harnessing the new team. The stop would last 30 minutes, just enough time for the stage passengers to eat, stretch and wish they were already to their destination.

Tuc and Jake stayed on the far side of the stage, watching the horizon and scrub brush covered desert before them for any sign of movement, wary of any foe.

Jake spit expertly and casually between his feet, leaning against the thin shade of the vehicle's side

"Get any sleep?" he had the gall to ask.

Tuc snorted in response, glaring at him from under the brim of his hat.

"Shit, no," he kicked a rock out into the brush and looked to the east.

There was an amiable silence between the two men. Both watched a collared lizard skirt from one bit of shade to another.

"What are you going to do with the money?" Tuc asked quietly. He could see Jake look sideways at him and smile.

"I'm going to spend it," he whispered happily.

"On what?" Tuc wasn't giving up.

Jake actually took a moment to think about his response. "A place. My place."

Tuc nodded. He understood.

"You?" Jake spit again.

"A wife."

Jake laughed out loud. It wasn't the answer that tickled him, it was at how quickly Tucker gave it.

"Yep. That will take it all. Make an honest man out of ya."

They both looked off into the distance again and smiled. A thin line of dust rose on the horizon. They both shifted towards the sight.

"Ready?" Jake asked.

"Yep."

They stood up straight and drew their guns. Jake looked at Tuc and winked. Both men began yelling and shooting randomly into the desert.

On cue Scott rallied also, whooping and raising his arms, startling the horses to safety. Drawing his guns, he followed suit. The three men moved into position to defend the oncoming attack.

"BUENAS DIAS, SEÑOR DESANDIEGO," Don Juaqin stood from a wingback hide covered chair behind a large hand carved desk, smiling warmly at the old man entering the room.

It was a study, same white stucco walls as the guest room, with high windows and a cool tile floor. There were books on shelves in the wall, more stacked on the tables and others in neat piles in the corners. No lamps were lit, but the room was light. Green plants grew happily in clay pots in the morning sun.

Again with the formal greeting, thought Y. "Buenas Dias," he offered his host cautiously.

"I trust you rested comfortably last night." It was a statement of fact not an inquiry. Y stood silent. He knew this peacock of a man would eventually tip his hand.

Santos Juaqin continued to smile as he came to the old man. Pausing for a moment to look him in his one good, very blood shot, eye. Y returned the stare.

"I have some maps," Don Jauqin finally offered after a lengthy pause. He turned on his heal back to the desk and the large parchments that lay there. He motioned for Y to come.

Y obliged. He knew what game they were about to play. He had played it with other treasure hunters. What was one more hand?

The parchments were mostly of the nearby Catalina Mountains. Some had marked trails and a system of x's, some he had seen before, some he had not, some were very old, maybe even as old as Y. Don Jauqin smoothed them across the desk top. He touched them tenderly as if they were very precious. Y glanced at his face. He already knew the next move.

Santos Juaqin wanted the Silver Door treasure he had

asked about the night before. He would do anything for it and he needed Y to help make it happen.

"I have all the maps that exist about the treasure we spoke of...the Silver Door Mine." Don Jauqin brought one map to the front of the pile and pointed to a spot high in the mountains. "I have heard many tales, but yours are the closest to what I have found in the maps. You have been there. You are the only one alive who knows exactly where it is. You are a living link to find this treasure, Señor DeSantiago." Santos paused waiting for a response.

Y rubbed his whiskered chin, looked at the map, nodding as he helped his eye follow the marked trail with his crooked finger.

Finally he said, "What do you propose, Señor?"

Don Juaquin clapped in anticipation.

"A partnership, my old friend!" He put his arm around the thin shoulders of the frail Yesidro. "You and I. We will find the treasure and we will both be wealthy."

It appeared to Yesidro that this man, Santos Juaqin, was already wealthy. A fine hacienda, guest quarters, servants, books. He had seen this before, too. Wealthy men wanting more wealth, risking all that they already had to find more. It was a sickness, it overcame them, possessed them, and ruined them. He also knew that it could not be cured. If he refused this man, Don Juaqin would kill him. If he went along with him, whether they found the treasure or not, he would also kill him. He thought quietly for several more minutes. Don Juaqin waited.

Yesidro wasn't afraid to die. For a few more moments he contemplated what little life he had left and what it afforded him. Why not die trying? He nodded, agreeing with himself.

Slowly, he offered his hand to the younger man, "It is a deal. Amigo."

9

―――――

Pitch black smoke curled slowly up her legs then up around her shoulders, pinning her to the ground. It was heavy, thick and greasy, she couldn't move from under it. There was a presence to this smoke, a chilling agenda. Growing thicker, it began to twist around her middle, up her torso, squeezing her lungs and moving to her neck.

She panted desperately. She was being suffocated, drowned by this filthy mass. She tried to struggle but didn't have the strength, tried to scream but didn't have the air, tried to cry but didn't have the tears.

She was so tired, so cold. She couldn't go on. She would just let it take her, it would be so much easier to just stop fighting. The smoke seemed to sense her weakness. It shuddered with anticipation and quickened in its movement. The blackness beckoned, it was so appealing, so still, so calm. At last she could rest.

There was a violent shuddering. Bev's body convulsed under the blackness, breaking through to an excruciating light. She choked and felt a sharp pain in her side. Every

nerve ending sparked and she flashed back into consciousness, eyes rolling wide open.

"Auugh," she cried out in fatigue and pain, gasping for
air. She was so weak, but still clawed at the space in front of
her trying to breath. Through blurry eyes she could see Sam
kneeling beside her, his hands were on his knees, his head
hung, he was openly weeping, shaking violently himself.

Bev raised her hand instinctively to comfort him. "What
happened? What's wrong? Are you all right?"

He laughed through the snot and tears that covered his
face. Wiping his mouth and nose off with his uninjured
hand, he took a deep breath.

He looked at her for a long moment before speaking,
"You collapsed, and stopped breathing." He rolled to the
ground beside her, spent.

"What?" Bev glanced around, it was all she could do to
roll her head sideways, her whole body ached. Suddenly the
whole horrible memory returned.

The shooting. Tara and Steve dead. Sam finding her.

They had walked a couple of miles to the police jeep
that Sam had been using to tail a drug ring through the
Arizona desert. They had been too late, someone else had
gotten there first, cut the fuel line and kidnapped Sam's
partner, B. Or worse.

Gathering what they could they found Bev some clothes,
and fled into the desert. Sam was certain they were fast
behind them. He had circled back several times and
watched their trail.

Bev had struggled to keep up, lack of food, little water
and the shock of the day had finally taken its toll. She had
collapsed.

"Seriously? Not breathing?" She winced, he must have

bruised her rib in saving her. He nodded, taking a huge breath himself. "Who are these people? Are you sure they're after us?" She was still trying to reason even in her desperate state.

"They're upper level cartel. Mule drivers. Cocaine. My partner and I have been following them for three months. If we had succeeded in capturing and interrogating them we would have had an in to one of the biggest drug rings in Southern Arizona. You and your friends walked right into the middle of a drop."

They both continued to lay exceptionally still, just breathing.

"Your partner...." she started to inquire. Without warning he quickly rolled over and put his hand over her mouth, signaling to be quiet. Terror rose again and her thumping heart pounded against sore ribs.

The desert was turning purple in the dimming light of dusk. Sam lay halfway over her like an animal protecting a wounded cub. He watched into the desert beyond them, barely breathing.

Then she heard it, too. A rustle, a whisper of movement beyond the shadows of the shrubbery. They would surely find them, they were right there in the wide open. She closed her eyes, not wanting to see the face of the oncoming terror.

The sound got nearer and more pronounced. It was foot-steps, several. She could hear them breathing and then a strangled whimper. Sam jumped up. Bev opened her eyes, what was he doing?

"B!?" Sam whispered hopefully. There was another yip from the quickening darkness. "B," Sam commanded. Bev didn't understand.

Suddenly a large four legged shape leaped into view

with an exuberant bark. Sam laughed and grabbed the German shepherd's neck.

"Oh my God, B! I thought they got you!" He sat on the ground to check her for wounds and greet her, accepting her sloppy kisses.

A dog...B was a dog.

"Oh my God," Bev finally clued in. "B is a dog."

B darted towards her then changed her mind and leaped back towards Sam.

"Okay, okay. Settle. Sit." B did as she was told, but her tail thumped in undeniable joy. "Yes, B is a narcotics dog. My partner." He petted her and scratched behind her ears. B was completely unhurt.

"Huh," Bev chuckled causing her rib to twinge.

All this time she had envisioned some dark skinned city coppette, busting out of her uniform, laughing and flipping her silken brown hair, sitting beside Sam in the tiny modified mustang cop car, drinking coffee together, defying death together and sharing all of life's important moments.

B came to Bev and licked her chin, looking into her eyes with what seemed to be her own knowing soul.

"Hi B," Bev responded and pet the dog.

B moved to lay beside Bev, putting her head across her stomach, sensing Bev's physical needs. B took a deep dog breath, relieved to be at her post. She settled in to do the job she was trained to do best, protect them both.

BEV COULD FEEL the synchronized rhythmic breathing of the man at her back and the canine at her front. She had slept soundly, a deep, black, thoughtless sleep. The light was beginning to change in the east, day was coming again.

The ground was not her friend. It bit into her shoulders and hips, but she was cautious not to move and disturb her guardians. She was surprisingly warm and felt incomprehensibly safe. She was just beginning to doze back off when B stiffened and let out a nearly indiscernible growl. Sam immediately responded by tightening his grip around Bev's middle and lifting his head to see over she and the dog.

"Stay," he whispered to them both as he eased up to his haunches, gun in hand.

The night before they had backed themselves up to a boulder on a small rise, a rarity in the desert, giving them a small advantage. They were at least protected on one side and could view the desert floor before them.

Sam scanned the horizon. He signaled for she and B to move back to the rock behind him, handing Bev his other weapon as they did.

The dog's hackles where raised, her nostrils flared, she kept silent but completely alert, acting as intensified senses for her partner. Sam instinctively followed the twitch of her ears and where she was watching in the scrub. She and Sam froze simultaneously watching one place off to their right, Bev followed their point.

There in the grey light, in the shrub, she saw a flash of light, a white shirt or hat perhaps. It moved in a familiar rhythm of a man walking. The figure was in no hurry, it had the deliberate gait of one following a known trail.

Sam signaled to the dog to go left. B silently went off into the scrub to flank the on-comer. Sam moved to go right signaling to Bev to watch the figure in the shrubs.

"Shoot to kill," he whispered before he moved away.

Shit, she thought. She sat up against the rock, never losing sight of the white marker in the bushes ahead. Whoever it was would walk right into Sam in moments.

Before she fully processed the many possible outcomes to the scenario in front of her, there were three sharp pops to the right. The white marker disappeared into the grey grasses under the shrubs.

Her heart slammed inside of her chest. There were no other sounds, none human or canine. She waited for what seemed like an eternity, then suddenly Sam and B burst through the shrubs side-by-side at a purposeful jog.

"We've got to move on," Sam instructed when he got close enough. "How are you feeling?"

"I'm fine, I can walk." Bev stood to prove herself. "Who was he?"

"Probably a tracker, he's dead." Sam looked in the opposite direction from where the assailant had come.

"When they don't hear from him they'll know we're still out here. We need to keep moving. We should be back to the field station tonight. It's farther than going back to Tucson, do you think you can make another 15 miles?"

B sat next to her, pressing her weight into her leg. Bev stroked the smooth head of the now smiling dog.

She smiled back, "Yes, I can make it."

Sam nodded. They gathered their gear and walked silently, single file into the desert.

10

———

Six dark men on skinny lathered mounts rode recklessly towards the Maricopa stage stop. Jake, Scott and Tuc were positioned between the oncoming hoard and the precious human and gold cargo they were paid to protect.

They heard the frightened commands of men's voices, the scrambling of furniture barring windows and doors as well as the shrill panic of a woman's voice in the stage house behind them. The banditos kept coming. As they crossed through the first gate in a cloud of dust, they split up, two to the left, two to the right and two coming head on, never slowing their pace.

Tuc saw the wild yellowed whites of their tortured horse's eyes, spurred on by the desperate men in their saddles as they approached. One of the mounts was foaming bloody spittle from its nose and mouth. Tuc glanced at Scott, knowing that the abuse would not go unnoticed by the horseman. These were men with nothing to lose.

Jake signaled the other two men with the nod of his head, indicating to stay in position. They had a plan.

They watched the two central riders clatter past, the other four would be behind the stage house by now. The horses skidded to a stop, knees buckling. The men flew off and headed to the cover of the water trough and paddock fence, weapons drawn. They hadn't seen the three men laying in wait at their back.

For a moment, the dust settled. One of the Mexican's horses wheezed frantically and turned to find water. The other collapsed completely, choking to death on its swollen tongue.

Scott made a move towards the beast. Tuc caught his arm, they couldn't give up their position yet.

"Damn," the driver hissed and stopped, keeping his head and holding his position.

Just as the horse expired there was a commotion to the back of the stage house. Men were yelling in English and Spanish, then the sound of shotgun fire. The passengers and stage stop owners were making a stand against the intruders in the back. On Jake's cue the three of them stood and silently moved in behind the two Mexican's hiding in the front.

All three men fired, shooting their two targets in the back. Scott fired two extra rounds into the back of their heads for general good measure then he shot the horse at the trough that was struggling to breathe, it crumpled thankfully to its death. He checked to see that the horse in front of the house was dead.

They waited. Shots continued to volley from the back. Suddenly one of the Mexicans ran around the side of the building. Jake leveled his gun and shot him mid-stride. He fell next to the horse at the trough. Scott spit in approval.

Silence fell again. Tuc listened. There was some movement in the house. A woman was crying. This was the part he wasn't looking forward to. The front door opened slowly, one of the men from the stage called out.

"Mr. Layton? Mr. Montgomery?" he asked cautiously.

"Yes," Jake answered keeping his position. "Three down out here."

"We got the other three in the back. I have two dead and one wounded inside."

Damn, Tuc thought to himself.

The stage house owner hobbled onto the porch behind the man speaking, he had been hit in the leg. Jake stepped out from the paddock, Scott and Tuc followed. The men at the house lowered their weapons.

Without pausing, Jake shot them in seconds. The woman inside screamed. There had been three stage passengers and the stage house owner and his wife inside. Jake was over the bodies and through the door before the woman had time to process what was happening. He shot her just as she raised the doubled barreled shotgun at the doorway.

Tuc paused, he had hoped that the banditos would have shot the woman, less on his and Jake's conscience. Nonetheless, it was done. The money was theirs.

The three men left the bodies where they lay. They put the four remaining nags that the Mexicans had ridden in on in the paddock, taking three fresh mounts for themselves and four more to give the appearance that the Mexicans had taken the horses and the gold. There was no one left to tell the tale.

Jake shot the hinges off the Wells Fargo strong box. The gold coin was a beautiful sight. Enough to keep ten men in luxury the rest of their lives. All three men grinned like boys as they divided the treasure into saddle bags and packed it onto their mounts. They moved quickly and efficiently as they all had a lot of ground to cover by nightfall.

It had been agreed on that they would split up. Scott was headed south to Mexico with the extra horses, Jake on to California and Tuc was going back to Texas territory. If the calvary or any hired tracker tried to follow them they would have to have three times the man power. This was unlikely.

Jake shook Scott's hand pulling him close to slap him on the back.

"Thank you, Willson."

"Pleasure." Scott swung himself into the saddle and tipped his hat. Tuc and Jake watched him move away.

He turned with a last wave and had just begun to lead the ponies out of the gate when the shot rang out.

Tuc jumped despite knowing it was coming. He saw the smoke from Jake's gun out of the corner of his eye. Scott Willson's silver grey pony tail gradually turned deep red under the back of his wide brimmed hat and he slumped forward as if in slow motion. His horse stopped, confused by his rider's position. Willson slowly slid off his saddle, his body landing in an awkward pile among the feet of the animals.

"Hmm," Jake holstered his gun. Tuc hung his head taking a deep breath. He had liked the man.

The two friends pulled themselves into their saddles. Jake stopped at the gate and untied the two saddle bags from Scott's horse, tossing one to Tuc. The bag seemed exceptionally heavy in his hands.

"Tuc?" Jake inquired of his friend. "You all right?"

"Yeah, yeah," Tucker Montgomery leveled his gaze at his long time brother, partner and compadre. "See you back in Texas." He managed a grin.

Jake winked, "Can't wait to meet the wife."

They parted company riding in completely different directions.

DON SANTOS JUAQUIN spent the better part of the next two weeks preparing for the trek into the desert. He encouraged Yesidro to study the maps in his office which Y thought was unnecessary.

The rest of Yesidro DeSantiago's time was spent enjoying the hospitality of his host. He hadn't been this comfortable, well fed or sober in many years. His burro, too, was fatter and more content than ever. Y took him apples and carrots from the kitchen when he could manage to sweet talk the cook.

"For you old man." He offered the beast the treat. The burro sniffed and gladly chomped down on the apple. "What do you think of all this?" Y gestured to the surroundings.

The burro chewed loudly, blowing air through his nose.

"Si, si! I know. It is not the wild desert life we are used to, huh?" He handed the carrot to the animal. "A gilded cage is still a cage, is it not? We are getting soft. I could use a drink."

Y sighed and so did the burro.

"Soon my friend, soon, we will be back on the rugged trails we love. One last adventure for us both." He smiled and scratched the mane between the animals ears. "Soon."

11

————

Desert hiking had lost all of its allure. Bev could no longer see the beauty in her surroundings. No color, no scent, no vista impressed. One foot in front of the other, one breath inhaled and expelled. It was all she could manage. She knew she was in shock from the last twenty four hours, her side ached, her head throbbed, and mentally she tried to push through. Every time she felt exhaustion overwhelming her she would glance at the shaggy dog beside her.

B trotted faithfully on, tongue lolling to one side or another, matching Beverly's pace, pausing when she slowed and turning when she lagged. The dog inspired. She and the dog followed Sam without hesitation or question. They all pressed on.

Sam made frequent stops. It wasn't particularly hot, 85 mid-day, but he knew that they were all suffering from the extreme situation. Keeping hydrated would keep them all moving. It was slow going, but necessary.

"How is your side?" he asked Bev at one of these rest breaks.

She took a sip of water from the gallon jug and managed a smile, "I don't think it's broken, just bruised." She could tell he was feeling bad about hurting her. "You saved me. I'll take a bruised rib any day. How's your hand?" After all she had wounded him as well.

He held it up for her to see, it was black with dirt and blood. Nasty. "I'll live." He grinned back. "I figure now you owe me."

"Really..." That grin. How could he be that attractive with everything they had just been through? "How about you get me out of this alive and in one piece and we'll talk about it."

He reached over and squeezed her shoulder, pulling her up gently as he stood.

"Deal." He kissed her cheek.

A jolt like an electric shock moved through her body. She wasn't dead yet. Bev's steps were lighter and she couldn't stop grinning for the next several miles.

THE BORDER PATROL outpost was a typical low lying government issued building, made of concrete and painted a dull beige. If not for the two black jeeps parked in front it would have been surprisingly difficult to see.

Bev, B and Sam had stopped a quarter mile from the building and were hidden in some greasewood. Sam watched through a small pair of binoculars. The two men they had seen go into the front door were dressed in desert camo and heavily armed. They were not Border Patrol or special narcotics police. That had been over 40 minutes ago. There had been no movement since.

"Well, it's obvious that they're waiting for something or

someone," Sam rationalized out loud. B listened intently, cocking her head slightly as if asking what the statement meant. "I think we'll wait too," Sam answered. The dog rested her head on her paws, content to do just that.

Bev couldn't help but notice their uncanny understanding of each other. B watched Sam's every move, her eyes never left him for long. When he spoke she strove to understand and obey any command. She checked their surroundings for his safety and read his need for touch and companionship. Pure devotion. If more women treated their men that way what a wonderful world it would be, for men perhaps. Bev smiled at the thought. She noticed Sam looking at her with a puzzled look.

"What?" she whispered

"You amaze me." His sincerity startled her. "All that's happened in the past 36 hours and you're still smiling." He smiled back

"Hmm, think how chipper I'll be after we get out of this." She sat down close beside him and leaned into his shoulder. She closed her eyes against the sunshine and breathed in the smell of his sweat, dust and greasewood baking in the heat.

She was dozing off when he whispered, "Here they come."

Bev looked off towards the horizon where a thin trail of dust was rising. It took a moment before the vehicles were visible.

"Look's like two SUV's," Sam reported.

Two, once black now dust covered, suburbans moved slowly along the sandy road. They were too far away to make any sound and the wait seemed endless to the three undercover.

At last they pulled in next to the jeeps. More armed men

piled out of the back seats. Five total. Bev noticed Sam taking note of each one, height, firearms, ethnicity. Finally the drivers, dressed in black suits, exited and each walked around to the passenger side of their vehicle. The movement was nearly synchronized, like a well practiced dance. The military men stood guard, scanning the horizon, ready to fire.

At one point, one of them seemed to be looking directly at them, but didn't react. *They obviously aren't looking very hard*, she thought.

Two people stepped out of the passenger side of the the vehicles. One was another dark skinned man in a black suit, distinguished from the drivers only by the attention he was receiving from the entourage. The other was a woman. She was slender and long and was also dressed in black, reminding Bev immediately of a feline. She was not prepared for the terrain. Her high heels and narrow skirt were better suited to a Manhattan office, and caused her to teeter unflatteringly into one of the soldiers. He caught her and virtually lifted her to higher more secure ground.

"Who are they?" Bev whispered.

Sam continued to monitor them through the binoculars. The V.I.P.'s were being escorted into the building.

"If I'm not mistaken," Sam finally lowered the binoculars "It's Fransisco Corrales. He's the president, if you will, of one of the largest cartels in Mexico. He's escaped prison twice because he owns the government, the prisons and most everything else in his country." He sighed, contemplating.

"And the woman?" It had not escaped Bev's attention that she was very beautiful and at least half the age of the drug lord.

"Could be his assistant, might be his lover, but my best

guess is that is his daughter, Carlotta Corrales. He's grooming her to take over."

"How thoughtful."

Bev wondered at the world and how screwed up it was. Because of the lovely twenty something Carlotta the drug queen, two people were dead and she and Sam had nearly died. She was sure they were all at the bottom of a very long list of destruction left in the cat-like Carlotta's wake. She instantly hated her, hated what she was, what she was doing and why.

"We have a unique opportunity here," Sam interrupted Bev's thoughts. "They're virtually alone, compared to how they're usually guarded. We have a chance to take out the current and future cartel leadership. Kill the two headed snake." His voice got more rapid and determined as he spoke. Bev saw something change in his eyes, something primal and somewhat violent.

She hesitated.

"There are two drug lords and nine armed men guarding them," she said, trying to be a voice of calm and reason. "We should go for help…"

Before she could finish, Sam was up, B at his heals.

"There will never be another time like this, with the two of them together." He was packing what little gear and water they had.

"But Sam, there are 11 of them." She had stopped in her tracks to drive home the point that she was making a stand against the idea.

"I have a plan," he said calmly as he turned back to her and reached out his hand for hers. He waited. "Trust me."

He had saved her so many times already. What could she do? She looked a B, who would blindly follow him anywhere. The dog trusted Sam and Bev trusted him, too. Besides, she sure as heck wasn't staying out her alone. She took his hand.

12

———

Father Miguel bowed with the humble gathering around the gravesite. Shadows from the ancient live oak moved across the pile of cobblestone as the dead danced for a moment in celebration, welcoming the neophyte to eternity.

"In the name of the Father, the Son, and the Holy Spirit, Amen." He crossed himself and looked up at the grieving family.

Juan Carlos Rodriquez had been in a confrontation that had ended in gun fire and had ended his life. His wife and four small children were now left without husband, father or support. The gunman was said to have been a stranger passing through, a searching gold miner, probably agitated by his losses and deficiency of luck. He was long gone and now many lives would be altered because of his wantonness. This was the very thing that Father Miguel had sensed was stirring. Now it was becoming reality.

The oldest boy, Juan Carlos Jr., was nearly 12. Too young to take on real responsibility, but old enough to feel the anger of unnecessary loss and realize the finality that death brought. Padre Miguel had offered to take him in. He would come to live at the boys school at the mission, perhaps become an acolyte in the church, maybe find his calling within its walls. That would help relieve the widow's burden of child rearing and perhaps save the child from using his rage less productively.

The priest moved next to him and put his arm around the boy's shoulders. Juan Carlos looked up with sad, dark questioning eyes.

"It will be all right, son."

The child's eyes showed disbelief. His mother stood on the other side of him and quietly cried into a lace hanky. She nodded to the boy when he looked her way.

"Si, Padre," he managed.

Father Miguel made his quiet condolences to the widow and her small children leaving them to the care of the other parishioners.

"Come, Juan. I will show you to your new room and you can meet the boys."

Juan glanced once more at his mother, who was now occupied with Juan's baby brother.

"Si, Padre." He turned with the Father and they made their way across the courtyard of the mission church.

WHITE DUST CARRIED by the heat of the canyon swirled in tiny spirals up and over the haunches and withers of the ancient one eyed burro. He groaned with each step of his tiny sure footed hooves, making his way up the canyon trail, his nose drooped into the trail of the horse's tail in front of him, one step in front of the other. Day after day for the past eight days the trail had been the same. Always the same.

The assembly consisted of Don Santos Jauquin, Y and ten other vaqueros from the ranch, their mounts and their pack animals. The clatter of hooves and the dust never ended. Y was not accustomed to horseback, he preferred to travel these hills on foot, but Don Santos had insisted. So with a nagging sense of vertigo and a sore ass, Y followed on the trail behind his new jefe, and Y's burro followed behind them.

"You know what they say old man?" he whispered to the burro over his shoulder. "If you aren't the lead horse the scenery never changes." Y chuckled at the beast with his head tucked in the tail of the bay mount. The burro blew his nose and wasn't amused.

Y, still grinning at his own humor, wrapped the reins around the saddle horn in front of him. The horse continued to plod in a stupor, following the path of the horse before him.

Y took a moment to look at his surroundings, the outcroppings, the arroyos. They were headed the right way. He took a drink from his canteen and readjusted his bony backside in the saddle. The days of this endless plodding had seemed like an eternity, but he had been through worse.

The heat and rhythm of the beast below him began to lull him to sleep. As it often does with old men, his mind drifted back to another trek through these mountains. A time when he and the burro were full, in flesh, in life and in sight. He sighed mindlessly at the thought of youth spent, let his chin rest on his chest, and dreamed...

Deep green dappled shadows blanketed the floor of the narrow valley, moving quicker in the flicker of creek where he and the beast had chosen to make camp. Y used the cottonwood tree as a pillow, dozing peacefully. His burro, grazed rhythmically nearby.

They had made their claim two days ago on a silver vein that was a quarter mile up the southeast canyon from this little oasis. In an effort to keep anyone from finding their treasure, Y camped away from the mine sight. There weren't many travelers in these canyons and none knew them as well as Yesidro, but if there were eyes watching he didn't want to tip his hand. The initial play at the mine had thrilled him. With a lot of hard work, a little stealth and a little luck Y would be a very rich man. He grinned to himself. Tomorrow the work would begin, but now he rested.

He hadn't slept long when the tinny sound of thin distant voices cut through his subconscious and startled him awake. The burro had stopped eating and was standing alert, his long rabbit ears pointed across the valley. The shadows were deep, filling the canyon slowly with the color purple.

Y sat up and listened intently. Sound carried long distances in these rocky arroyos especially in the still of early evening. The burro still watched. Several minutes passed. Only the evening bird songs and the slight sounds of water broke the silence.

The burro eased his stance and went back to pulling on the green grass. Just to be sure, Y decided not to build a fire this evening, it would be cold tack for dinner. He stood and stretched. He would take a leak then go get some water from the creek.

The shot rang out, its echo down the canyon had almost finished its reverberation when he felt the sting in his back right shoulder. The impact spun him around and into the tree. Out of the corner of his eye he saw the burro jump and bolt for cover. He decided to do the same.

Scrambling, the two of them headed for heavy brush

along the creek bed. The burro crashed through the water and into the brush on the other side. Y decided to stay on the closer bank. He lay in the mud, breathing heavily, trying to assess the situation.

The shot had come from the west. The pain in his shoulder began to push through the adrenaline rush. He fingered the wound. The bullet had passed through, probably shattered his upper shoulder blade and his collar bone. Groaning, he ripped pieces from the bottom of his shirt and packed the wound, then tied his now useless arm up against his chest.

Damn. It was his shooting hand.

Y took the pistol out of his holster and, holding it at his hip, loaded it then placed it in his left hand. He sat perfectly still, slowed his breathing and waited.

It was nearly dark when he heard the first scream. It was close, behind him and it wasn't human. His adrenaline surged again, heart throbbing in his wound and pounding in his chest and ears. He turned to find the source. There in the not too far distance was the yellow glow of a fire.

How had they gotten around him? Another scream brought him to his feet. It was a horse, someone or something was wounding a horse. He moved carefully through the brush to have a clear view. The animal suddenly let out another sound, a very familiar sound, a bray that Y knew better than any human voice.

"Oh Dios," he prayed. His burro.

On the other side of the creek he could see through to the camp sight. The movement, the pain and the sounds made his head swim and he retched.

Three banditos had his burro hobbled and tied at the neck. The animal heaved and struggled under the restraints. Y could see blood streaming down the animal's face. They had taken his eye and were cutting the tendons at the back of his hooves.

On impulse, Yesidro jumped through the hedge and ran the 20 yards to the edge of the firelight. The scene unfolded in slow motion. He was halfway across the expanse when the men turned.

They were all grinning. They knew he would come. Y had the advantage of shooting from the dark into the light and although he was moving and using his bad hand he hit one of them in the head, killing him where he stood. The other two returned fire, letting go of the burro who fell to the ground.

It took two shots to bring Y down, one to the knee and one to the side. The men drug him to the burro and threw him down on the beast.

"You fool," snarled the shorter stockier Mexican. "You would lose your life for this beast?" He kicked at the burro's hindquarters. The animal didn't move, just panted as it went into shock.

Y stroked the burro's neck under him and whispered, "Stay with me friend, I'm going to need your help."

Both men laughed. The taller thinner man spit. They pulled Y up and tied his arms behind him causing him to lose consciousness for a moment from the pain in his shoulder. Once they had him secure the stocky one put his face an inch from Yesidro's.

"Where is your play?" He waited for Y's answer.

When it didn't come fast enough he stood and back handed the wounded man across the face. Y fell over with a yelp.

"We know you made a claim in town. We have followed you for two days."

Y tried to think fast, it was increasingly difficult with the radiating pain and the loss of blood.

"My pocket" he finally whispered, he could see no other way out. Maybe if he gave them what they wanted, they would leave Y and the burro to die. And then maybe they wouldn't. Either way, Yesidro felt sure this was the day he would die.

The taller man fished through the blood soaked shirt and found the document from the assayer's office making claim to the silver vein up the valley. Yesidro watched him inspect it upside down with all the insight of a baboon. The tall thin man couldn't read. He handed it to his companion, who was able to surmise the correct direction of the document, but his puzzled look indicated he didn't speak or read English. The bandits had obviously not considered any of this. Yesidro had a chance.

"I can read it to you," he offered through his split lip.

The men hesitated, dumbfounded by the whole situation.

The stocky man snarled, "How do we know you are telling us the truth?" But even as he said it, he brought the document closer to Yesidro.

"Leave me here alive until you find the mine. If you find it you leave me, let me live. If I lie you can come back and kill me." Yesidro could feel the slow steady heartbeat of the still burro beneath him, they weren't dead yet.

The two men looked at each other and shrugged. What choice did they have?

"Read it, en español."

Yesidro read the directions to the mine to the men translating it into Spanish. They made him repeat it three times to make sure his story didn't change. Finally satisfied, they stepped to the other side of the fire and conversed in low tones that Yesidro couldn't hear. Contemplating his fate no doubt and whether they should follow the instructions given. They would have to wait until morning to start out anyway.

Yesidro took a deep breath. His side and shoulder had stopped bleeding, his knee was shredded, the pain miraculously had subsided, a benefit of shock and blood loss. He hung his head and prayed until blackness took over.

Morning came with a jolting kick from the tall thin bandito. Yesidro yelled, cursing in Spanish, forgetting for a moment where he was and what was happening.

The two men were preparing to leave for the mine sight. Before he could clear his head, both men were on top of him holding him down. The stocky man unsheathed his knife and without ceremony shoved it into Yesidro's eye socket.

A new wave of pain unlike anything he had ever known pierced his head, neck and spine. He thought he was screaming, but couldn't hear any noise. The burro began to thrash with the smell of fresh blood and the struggle. When the men let Yesidro go he was head down on the ground, pressing his face into the rocky soil for some sort of relief, heaving in pain.

"If we have to come back, we will take your other eye, asshole, but not before we skin your beast alive while you watch. Then we will kill you." They mounted their horses and rode past.

The man and beast waited until the clatter of hooves was distant then they both began rolling in their own blood and urine, making nearly the same guttural sounds, attempting to free themselves. Both recognized that now was the time to flee. Yesidro had not translated the document correctly, they would be back and he had no doubt they would make good on their threats.

The blood from Yesidro's wounds had soaked the ropes that bound him, they were slippery and with his last ounce of energy he pulled his hands free. The burro too had kicked and pulled until he had freed his back legs and was attempting to stand. Yesidro crawled to him and freed his front feet.

The burro stood, but his two cut tendons caused him to stumble. One back and one front hoof were disabled, his face and velvet muzzle matted with blood from the loss of his eye.

"Whoa, burro." Yesidro stroked the animal's neck as he sat beneath him. The burro settled, smelling Yesidro's face and shoulder, knowing that his master was also wounded. "If we work together my friend, we will live." The burro turned to use his good eye to see his companion, agreeing.

Yesidro pushed himself up using his one good arm and one good leg. He wrapped his good arm around the burro, who started at the pain in his feet, but then allowed the weight. One foot slowly after the other they made their way to the creek and down the valley like a mutant creature from some Spanish folk tale.

Yedisro hit the ground on his side, calling out in shock as he slide from the saddle. The procession stopped abruptly. The big bay horse stopped, instinctively waiting for his rider.

"Señor Yesidro!" Jauquin shouted and turned to assist the old man. Two of the other men behind had also dismounted to do the same.

Yesidro stammered and took the arms of the younger men. He dusted himself off, embarrassed. The younger men chuckled and got back to their horses. Señor Juaquin looked at him for a moment.

"Pardon, Señor . I must have dozed off." Yesidro

awkwardly remounted the bay. The group continued on.

In all the commotion no one noticed the loan rider that had been watching them for the last half hour on the ridge above.

He shifted in his saddle and contemplated where the convoy was headed.

Jake Layton chuckled to himself, "Poor old fool."

13

———

S am, Bev and B walked quietly and quickly along the ridge around to the far side of the border station. They stayed in the shadows of the Mesquite and Pallo Verde trees hoping to avoid detection from the armed guard below. Once they were aligned with the back of the building, Sam stopped, unloaded his pack and began to assemble gear and guns. He gave Bev a small pocketknife and a .22 pistol.

"Put the gun in your back waistband." He demonstrated with his own, pulling his t-shirt over the butt of the gun.

Bev had shot a gun at a range, but never in self-defense. Sam sensed her hesitation.

"Have you fired a gun before?" he asked matter-of-factly, no judgement.

"Yes." She handled the weapon and put it in her waistband. "Just never in a must kill situation."

"You have ten shots in the magazine, aim high in the chest. There's a good chance they're wearing body armor, but the recoil of the gun will cause you to hit high and you will nail them in the neck or head. If that doesn't work aim for the groin, it will stop them every time." He winked, but all humor was gone.

The plan was simple. Move in after nightfall, draw the guards out with a distraction, taking out as many without gunfire as possible. Enter the building and find and kill or, if possible, capture the Cartel King and Princess. Simple.

"Just like a Bond movie," quipped Bev.

"Yeah," Sam grinned broadly. "You can be Pussy Galore."

"Watch it." She grinned back. "I'm armed and hungry." Nerves were obviously getting the best of both of them.

"Hey," he said, suddenly serious again. He reached for her, drew her to him, and kissed her. Pulling away slightly, he said, "We've got this."

She nodded. He took her hand and they made their way down the side of the ridge and onto the desert floor behind the building.

It had been decided that Bev would be the distraction. She would see if she could lure several of the guards to a jeeping accident where her husband was badly injured. She certainly looked the part.

She was dirty, bloody, dehydrated and disheveled. She was not, however, a very convincing actress in her own mind and hoped that the nerves would come across as fear and shock to the unknowing audience. Hopefully the militants would be less threatened by a lone woman coming to them for aid and not kill her immediately.

Sam would be hidden about 50 yards up the arroyo that they had made their way down. Evening was coming and it would make it easier to ambush anyone who bought the ruse.

Bev took a deep breath and exhaled quickly, like she was preparing for a race. She was violently scared and felt like puking, but there was nothing in her stomach to expel.

"Now or never." She smiled weakly at Sam and patted B who whined, understanding that something was about to happen.

"I'm right here. I will back you up if something goes wrong." His words and his touch didn't really comfort her this time, she just wanted to get on with it.

She turned, ran down the narrow gulch and stumbled out into the open area behind the building. Motion sensor lights flashed on and she began to scream.

"Oh God! Please!"

The tears and tension came surprisingly easily. She poured all of her exhaustion into her act. She heard shouting from inside and the sound of arms engaging. She screamed again.

"My husband, he's dying...please!"

There were five heavily armed men in front of her within moments, she fell to her knees, begging. The men held steady.

"Oh God!" She looked up, crying hysterically now, her stomach and her rib hurt from her efforts. "Please, por favor!"

Another man came out of the house, perhaps the head guard. "Bajen sus amras," he commanded them.

Bev continued to weep, head bowed. They weren't going to shoot her yet. The men relaxed their stance. The head guard approached her. She looked up reaching for him.

"Por favor, Señor, mi esposo is....is dying."

He evaluated her just out of her reach, sizing her up. "What has happened Señora?" he finally asked.

"W-we were jeeping up the canyon." She pointed back towards where Sam was hiding. "We turned over....he's trapped...he's bleeding...please...I can't help him by myself." Tears flowed again.

He said nothing, but indicated by the twitch of his head for two of the men to assist her. She collapsed against them as the lifted her up. She hadn't thought about them frisking her, the gun was still in her waist band.

"Sanchez, Alvarado, Nuñez...via con ella."

They did not consider her a threat. The plan was working.

"Gracias, th-thank you," she stammered. "Please hurry!"

She knew that Sam was watching, but the ambush would be as much a surprise to her as to the guards. She tried not to act suspicious as she turned and led them back to the canyon.

If the men were apprehensive they didn't show it. They walked briskly behind her as she trotted up the narrow trail, guns slung over their shoulders behind them. There was a large boulder ahead that they would have to move around or climb over to continue on the trail and suddenly Bev could sense what was going to happen. She kept moving, no hesitation, one large step up and over the boulder. Then, using the last of her energy, she pushed off the rock and dove for cover.

Sam and the dog were on the men in seconds, leaping from the other side of the rock right into their faces. Sam slit one of their throats before his feet hit the trail and was on the second as B knocked the third down, going for his neck.

There had been no time for yelling, not even in surprise. The guards had been busy negotiating the boulder. All three now lay dead.

Bev dropped onto the trail, panting like a wild animal. Sam confiscated guns, ammo and pocket contents, and collapsed beside her with his spoils.

"We don't have long. You were great." He handed her the assault rifle and another larger knife.

B joined them. She looked much more ominous with a bloody muzzle and a rough, wild gleam in her eyes.

"Good dog." Sam patted her head and her countenance changed, returning to a pet rather than a weapon.

"Six guards and two drug lords to go," said Bev. "What now?" Her disregard for human life surprised her, but it was kill or be killed. She knew that, and that knowledge had shifted something in her psyche.

"We need to get close. It won't take long for them to wonder what has happened to these three and come looking. While they do that we'll have a chance of getting in. If they get spooked they will lock down the bosses, whisk them away, our window will close...and they'll kill us."

It was all so surreal. Sam stood and pulled Bev up beside him. They looked like militant vigilantes out of some spy movie. Bev half expected the anticipatory background music to start as they moved along the edge of the canyon in the deepening shadows.

She had to admit she felt empowered by the arms around her shoulder and tucked in the small of her back. There was a glimmer of confidence that they just might succeed pulling her forward. B tapped her hand with her muzzle in silent camaraderie, she believed it too.

14

———————

Jake made his way back to his camp, pondering the group of travelers he had encountered. After the stage robbery he had decided to make his way into Mexico with the extra horses. He had been cautious, taking the hardest trails and doubling back making sure he hadn't been followed. Convinced no one was after him, he was under no time constraints.

On his solo ride he had plenty of time to contemplate his future. He was considering settling south of the border, a large ranchero and a round, soft, warm Mexican wife the color of brown sugar. What could be wrong with that? His new found wealth would make him a prince in the old world.

Based on the gear the entourage carried they were planning on mining. These hills were rich with gold and especially silver. He wondered if they already knew their destination or were they only seeking? Maybe he should put in a few days investigation. He automatically began packing his camp.

"It might be worth it," he said out loud as he patted the

saddle bags already laden with his earlier cache. "Might be worth it."

<hr>

THE RANCH HANDS MADE quick work of setting up camp and getting the evening meal started. Don Juaquin had retired to his canvas tent to examine his maps and had made it clear that he wanted to speak to Yesidro after the meal.

Y had been content with the direction and the distance that they had covered, but he got the distinct impression that Don Juaquin did not share his analysis. Being rich and impatient made him ungrateful jefe. Yesidro liked him less and less.

He brought the burro a bucket of water, cussing his sore chaffed legs and ass.

"I am not made for a saddle Burro."

The burro sunk his muzzle into the water up to his nostrils and drank deeply. Y handed him an apple which the beast took, munching gratefully.

"You and I have seen some trails eh, Burro?" Y patted the dry dusty neck.

The burro didn't mind, instead he shifted his weight towards the old man in hope of more attention. Y smiled and scratched some more. How odd to have an attachment to such a lowly beast, but then again Y was just as lowly.

"A more wretched pair as there ever was." Yesidro turned to leave for his meeting.

Don Juaquin's silhouette was bent over the maps on his table inside the tent. The warm lantern light glowed around him and shown directly on his face giving it the appearance of a carved mask whose expression was hard, driven, demonic. Yesidro paused for a moment, knowing that the light was revealing this man's true inner being. He crossed himself instinctively.

"Buenos tardes, Señor," he stated as he finally entered the tent.

Don Juaquin turned, his mask melting into a welcome grin. "Come in my friend. Come and show me how we are doing on our adventure." He waved the old man to the table.

Yesidro did as he was told. The map was the one they had studied before.

Don Juaquin pointed. "We are here correct?" He tapped the map

"Si," Yesidro nodded.

"How much longer?" Don Juaquin glanced sideways at the old man, drawing his finger to the 'x' that had been sited and tapped again.

"It is rough terrain, Señor. Two days." Y was matter of fact.

Don Juaquin sighed deeply.

"The mine and its treasure aren't going anywhere." Y grinned and tried to lighten the jefe's mood to no avail. The younger man slammed his open hand on the map, causing the lantern flame to flicker. Y held his ground, still grinning slightly.

"Two days. And we shall know?" Don Juaquin glared at Y.

Yesidro nodded. "Two days," he confirmed and left Don Juaquin to his ire.

15

———

Three armed men from the group that had greeted Bev earlier stood outside the back of the building in a halo of yellow light that cut into the desert darkness. They smoked short cigarettes and spoke quietly in Spanish. They were not missing their compadres yet. One of them laughed, his voice louder than the other two.

Bev instinctively squatted behind Sam and B, staying low. Sam was considering scenarios in his mind, the dog alert and waiting. Just as Sam rose slowly to move forward, the back door flew open and he returned quickly to a crouch.

"Donde estan los hombres?" The men jerked to attention at the inquiry of El Capitán.

"No se, Capitán," one of them answered

El Capitán looked out into the darkness and it seemed to Bev like he looked directly at her. Logically she knew he couldn't see her, but her heart began that familiar pounding in her chest. The pounding reverberated in her head and her breathing became shallow. Fear rose instinctively.

"Encuentren ellos!" El Capitán commanded.

The men put out cigarettes and gathered their gear. They were coming out to look.

B growled, a low vibration, her hackles raised. Sam put a hand on the back of her neck and she went silent. They waited, poised to ambush the second wave of guards.

It seemed like an eternity for them to cross the 50 yards that spanned between them. For a moment Bev lost them in the haze of light that faded into the dark of the desert. If they continued their course they would pass not 15 feet in front of Sam, the dog and herself.

She tried not to hold her breath. Instead she took slow silent purposeful inhalations and exhalations, trying to calm herself down. The men were now dark shadow figures on a quickly darkening backdrop. One of them paused to turn on a flashlight.

"B and I will take the first two, you jump the third," Sam whispered over his shoulder not waiting for her response.

She had never had to kill anyone–wait…yes she had.

Fool, she thought, *yes, you have!"*

It had only been a few months since she had to fight off her would be killer in the hospital. The thought almost made her laugh out loud, but Sam rose silently and she checked back into the moment. Somehow this revelation did not inspire any more confidence.

"Get as close as you can to him, shoot at close range." That was the last instruction Sam gave, then he and B disappeared silently in front of her. She fought the urge to follow him and turned her attention to the last man on the trail.

Using all of her senses, she crept forward as silently and carefully as she could. She heard the shuffle of the men's boots on the gravel trail as they followed the pin point of light from the flashlight. She drew the gun from her waistband. When she was no more than ten feet from her prey, there was a disturbance to her right up the trail. The two men in front momentarily stopped and were confused, their flashlight flashing into the brush. She made her move.

With one arm she wrapped herself around the back of the third man, wrenching him sideways. He made a startled sound and she pushed the muzzle of the gun hard against his temple and fired. There was a flash and for a fraction of a second she could see the silhouette of his face–then it was gone.

He fell hard with her on top of him. Her ears rang from the shot, but she could sense movement around her so she scrambled off and into the shrubs for cover.

The splatter of blood, the smell of burning flesh, gunpowder and sweat overcame her and nausea hit again in a giant wave with dry, choking heaves. The brush of fur startled her at first, but she realized it was B and she steadied herself by holding onto the dog's ruff. Suddenly, Sam was pulling her up and they were moving.

As her head cleared she purposed her feet to move with him and could barely hear the commotion at the back of the building, the building they were heading directly towards. The gunfire had roused the rest of the guard and El Capitán was yelling and pointing to the vehicles.

Sam had been right, they were fleeing. He broke into a full run with B at his side. It would be hand-to-hand now.

She could finally hear the volleying gunfire in her ringing ears. She ran too.

Sam fired his gun as he moved, trying to stop the two men heading to the Suburban. Bev headed to the wall of the building just outside the flood light glare. With her back against the wall she panted and readied her rifle.

The yelling, gunfire and barking continued just out of her view beyond the other side of the wall.

"Shit!" she cursed between her teeth.

Then she heard it. A shuffle to her right, deeper in the shadow. Without thinking, she turned, braced the gun and fired. The momentary flash lit up three shocked faces in the dark, El Capitán, Francisco and Carlotta Corralles. The woman screamed and someone fell, but Bev didn't know who.

Before she could turn to flee, a figure lunged from the darkness. El Capitán tackled her, pinning her completely with his body weight and quickly enabling her rifle. He rose up just enough to slam the back of his gun across her face. The stars were short lived then all the ringing in Bev's ears stopped and there was only silent blackness.

16

On the evening of the second day, just as Y had predicted, the dusty treasure hunters plodded into the narrow river valley. Yesidro sat up in the saddle a little taller. It was the same valley that he and burro had been accosted in so many years ago. His senses were immediately more keen as if the danger somehow still existed. Burro, too, let out a disgruntled bray at the scent of the grass and water and perhaps some past recollection.

Jefe Don Juaquin raised his hand when he reached the creek edge. The company halted. He turned his horse and came to Yesidro's side.

"Are we close?" he asked harshly.

"Si, Señor. A quarter mile."

Don Juaquin turned again and shouted instructions to his men to make camp here for the night. They would go to the mine in the morning.

Yesidro dismounted and took a deep breath. How he wished for a drink. Something to dull the aches of mind and body. All his life he had thought of returning to the mine, of toiling to unearth the treasure. What had stopped him? Pride? Fear? Time? His face sagged, he felt very old.

He had forged such plans. A home, a wife, maybe children. The silver would have set him up for life. He would have lived like Don Juaquin, but appreciated it, shared it.

Instead he had hidden in the desert, in the bottom of a bottle, forever feeling the sting of defeat that he had felt from the banditos in this valley so long ago. He had pushed the memory deep plodding these dusty hills, circling around his prize but never daring to grab it. He wiped a tear from his cheek with the sleeve of his shirt.

"Damn, old man," he scolded himself. "I have been sober too long, Burro. I'm too clear headed." And with that Yesidro went to find a compadre who had packed tequila, leaving the burro to graze in blissful ignorance.

FOUR HORSEMEN WATCHED the thin blue line of campfire smoke from high on the canyon rim. They were strangers to this territory but not to this hunt. It had been a long ride, but they were used to that as well. Well trained seasoned professionals who were bound to protect, serve and bring the corrupt to justice. Under the shade of their wide brimmed hats and long oilcloth dusters all four wore the signet star of the Texas Rangers.

They watched the miners pitch camp and they also watched the other side of the canyon. The lone horseman with several spare ponies that had been following the company was himself being followed.

"Looks like everyone is holding up for the night. Let's do the same." Terrance Goodwin dismounted and the other three men followed suit in unceremonious silence.

They were closing in.

They had all agreed that Jake Layton was most likely planning another robbery. Layton already had armed robbery, the murder of three innocents as well as the cold blooded murder of a Texas guardsman and Marshall Scott Willson, one of their own, on his record. The west was wild, robbery and murder were common, these lawmen, however, were bound–bound to find justice for their fallen companion. That was the only legitimate reason they were authorized to hunt him down.

They were patient. They would wait.

They would give him enough rope to hang himself and capture him in one more act.

FATHER MIGUEL WATCHED the boys run and push after the crude rag ball using only their feet. The game was fascinating, feet flying and laughing, faces flashing white teeth. Juan was among them, not as skilled but trying. It made the pastor's heart glad to see him being a child, no cares, complete freedom from the burdens of life.

He sighed.

"It is how we are all supposed to be," he admonished himself. "Free from the burdens of this world, bubbling with joy for simple blessings. Forgive me Lord for not letting go, for trying to carry the weight. Praise You for carrying it for me." He bowed and crossed himself and continued to watch the game.

The ball flew to his feet. The boys encouraged and taunted him to join them. Father Miguel grinned broadly, stood and lifted his robes to free his feet. He gave the ball a swift kick and chased after it amidst shouts of glee from the children and astonished looks from some of his brethren.

"Joy from simple blessings," he panted as he ran, loving every second.

17

———

Air moved relentlessly making it difficult to catch her breath. The constant hot breath of an unseen monster blew from one direction, then the opposite. Bev could never get a fix on its location. She knew it was sinister without ever seeing its form. It taunted and twisted her like a bug caught in a web.

A tiny spark of light lit the pitch darkness with a flash. It flickered and moved with the air current. Bev twisted and searched in the dim illumination, but there was still no sign of her adversary. The spark grew quickly into a consuming blaze. She struggled to leave, but couldn't.

The fire crossed the floor beneath her and created a pitch black smoke, which curled slowly up her legs then up and around her shoulders. It was heavy, thick and greasy, she couldn't move out from under it. The smoke had presence, a chilling agenda. It grew thicker and began to twist around her middle, up her torso, squeezing her lungs and moving to her neck.

She panted desperately, terrified. She was being suffocated, drowned by this filthy mass. Heat rose from below.

She tried to struggle but didn't have the strength. Tried to scream, but didn't have the air. Tried to cry, but didn't have the tears.

She was so tired. She couldn't go on. She welcomed death.

The smoke seemed to sense her weakness and shuddered with anticipation, quickening its movements. The blackness beckoned, it was so appealing, so still, so calm. At last she could rest. Just rest.

"Just rest," said the voice, reverberating in her empty skull. She knew the voice and inclined towards it, if only in spirit. Spirit, it would seem, was enough. Her breathing calmed.

In the momentary calm, water dripped. She could hear it, she could smell it, her heightened senses driven by intense thirst. Bev could feel the water rolling down her skin. Regardless if it was real or not, it was a welcome relief to the fiery reoccurring nightmare in her mind.

She wanted to taste the water more than she had ever wanted anything. Where was it coming from? It seemed to be rolling from the wrong direction, coming from the center of her chest, rolling in a tiny stream between her breasts, over her throat and dripping off her chin.

She tried to open her eyes, tipping her chin to her chest to get her mouth closer. Then she was sure her eyes were open or almost open, yet she could see nothing but blackness.

When she finally did open her mouth she inadvertently let out a groan. She was certain of one thing....she was conscious.

She licked her chin, trying to lead the water to her mouth, every movement was an effort, every muscle was so heavy. It took several minutes, but Bev finally realized that she was upside down hanging from her feet.

The revelation caused a new wave of panic. She twisted around trying to free herself. The haze between her unconscious fears and her current reality blended in her mind. Her efforts were futile. It only took moments before she was completely exhausted, her body dropping like a hooked fish.

"Easy," she told herself out loud.

Her tongue was dry and her face felt stiff, like it was cracking. She could taste and smell blood. Moving her hand gingerly she touched her left eyebrow, wincing at what she felt. There was a large gash over her eyebrow. She could feel the torn jagged flesh and what might be smooth bone. Her eye was swollen shut and what she assumed was blood crusted along the side her face and into her hair. Her memory flashed to El Capitán and the butt of his rifle.

"God," she groaned, partially a prayer, partially in astonishment that she was still alive. How long had she been strung up like prize game? The thought plodded heavily through her cracked skull.

She had to get upright, her lungs felt heavy against her heart and it was beating uncharacteristically slow. Taking a deep breath she engaged every stomach muscle she ever had, wishing she had done extra crunches sometime in her life. Grabbing her calves, she held the 'v' sit for a few moments, allowing the blood to stop thumping in her head, relieving her heart. She let go and hung back down, the pain in her ankles was excruciating. Reaching up again, this time trying for her feet, she missed and fell back hard.

"Aaaugh," she shouted in pain, her voice echoing around the inky darkness.

Bev let her body stop swinging before she tried again.

Once more she lifted herself, finally finding her bindings. They were some sort of poly rope, not very thick, but wound around her ankles and feet at least four times. She eased herself back down and tried to wriggle her feet, they were not moving. They would have to be cut.

The knife! Sam had given her a knife.

Sam. Where was he?

Where was she?

Bev fumbled in one of her front pockets. Nothing. Then the other. For a moment her heart sank, she didn't feel anything. Then she realized the pocket was folded over due to her position and she dug further, finding the multi-bladed tool.

"Just don't drop it," she instructed herself.

Opening up one of the blades it felt large enough and sharp enough to do the job. Gripping it carefully, she pulled back up.

Blindness added an extra element to the process. She cut her own ankle several times and had to hang back down just as many. Her stomach muscles began to ache from her efforts, as did the rest of her body.

Half way through, the ropes shifted and it suddenly dawned on her that she had no idea where she was, or how high she was from any surface.

"Shit!" she called out in complete frustration.

Anger and fear welled up in her as the bindings became less and less stable. As they loosened she managed to wedge one foot against the other and push off her shoe. It fell past her face in the dark and in several seconds she heard it hit the ground below. The sound was sharp, obviously striking a hard surface, maybe 10 feet or more below her.

She held still and thought about her next move. Falling headfirst would be the least desirable. She had already endured enough blows to the head today. Could she cut the rope one handed and hang on as her feet came free? She doubted it, but there was really no other choice.

She took several deep breaths, pulled herself up once more and wrapped the rope around her free hand above her bound ankles.

"Cirque du Soleil watch out," she quipped.

Wedging the knife under the rope closest to her ankle, Bev began to methodically saw back and forth. It was tedious and seemed to take forever. Just as she was about to let herself back down to rest, there was a pop. One of the ropes had split.

Her body suddenly shifted causing her to gasp and grip the rope above her tighter. But she still wasn't free. Slowly she resumed the sawing, shoulders burning. She listened intently to the rope at her fingertips. It began as a ripping sound and another pop, then the rope let loose. The knife flew from her hand and she grasped wildly for a hold above her to stop her fall.

Her other shoe fell off as both feet broke free. Bev's grip held for maybe a second as her body weight jolted loose, then she was falling sideways into the pitch black. There was no time to yell out, and no one to hear her anyway.

The landing was crushing, causing a flash of light inside her head, the pain radiating through every nerve. The wind knocked out of her and she took short rapid breaths wanting to scream.

Instead she instinctively curled into a fetal position and right before she passed out she heard the voice again.

"Just rest."

18

____

The Rangers gathered quietly around the small fire. It would be extinguished before daylight to prevent detection from the camp below and across the valley.

Tuc squatted as close to the embers as his large frame would allow. Despite it being a fairly warm night, the dawn air chilled him. Perhaps it wasn't just the temperature, but the nagging feeling that had haunted him ever since Wells had solicited he and Scott Willson...and since Willson's death.

They had been working on the stage in the local blacksmith shop preparing for the long transit ahead. Willson was pounding out some of the coach's bent framework, beating it mercilessly. Tuc had been watching, drinking whiskey straight from the bottle, enamored with the sparks that flew from the collision of hammer and hot metal. The two men had been visiting about the job ahead, fielding general questions and concerns to one another. Just sharing pleasant company.

Tuc preferred the atmosphere of the barn to the rowdy

watering holes down main street where Jake spent his evenings. The air was cleaner, no tobacco smoke, no smell of sweaty men and women. Only dirt, hot metal and straw, and horses. Other than the din of the hammer it was quiet.

Tuc had just taken a deep breath and settled back against a large post when the banker entered, flanked by two strangers. Tucker immediately recognized them as Texas lawmen, Rangers. He had seen them on a couple of occasions during he and Jake's adventures in Texas.

Scott stopped his metal work, wiping his hands on a rag. Tuc stood and put his bottle down.

"What can we do for you gentlemen?" he asked sincerely.

The banker exchanged a knowing glance with his companions and moved closer.

"It is perhaps what we can do for each other," said Henry Wells.

Tuc and Scott moved towards each other, always cautious, until they were shoulder to shoulder facing their visitors. Both knew where their firearms were and where their guest's were as well, just in case.

"What would that be?" Willson asked, genuinely curious.

"Well," Mr Wells continued. "It seems we have a problem." He let the words hang in the air for effect.

"Problem? With the deal?" asked Tuc.

They were a week or so out from making the longest run across country for the well know bank. Tuc would hate for the job to go sour now. He needed the pay.

"Yes." The banker was firm and obviously concerned.

"How so?" Willson began to be concerned as well. He needed this job too.

"I see your companion, Jake Layton, is not around this evening."

The change of subject confused the two men being queried.

"Yes, sir. Shall I go find him? I believe he's down the street." Tuc's offer was stopped short by a flick of the banker's wrist. Tuc looked curiously at the Rangers knowing instinctively that his friend was in some sort of trouble.

"No, no... I think we can handle this without him. It does, however, have to do with him." The banker turned to the men by his side. "It has come to my attention, via these fine law men from Texas, that Mr. Layton is a wanted man."

Tuc furrowed his brow and took a deep breath. It was best to listen first and speak last with accusations flying. Scott Willson crossed his arms over his chest defiantly and also waited for further explanation.

Getting little reaction, the banker continued, "Mr. Montgomery, you are also charged in this matter."

The two men met each other's gaze.

Tuc responded, "Now wait a minute, what in the hell are you talking about?"

For the first time the red headed Ranger spoke from behind Henry Wells.

"My name is Marshall Terrance Goodwin, Texas Ranger." He spoke slowly and in a low Texas drawl, moving toward Tuc. "You and Mr. Layton are being charged with the murder of three Texas guardsmen during a shootout in San Salve canyon on May 25, 1885."

"What? Texans? They were all Mexicans! I'm sure of it." Tuc stood his ground, certain he and Jake were innocent. "I don't know where you got your information, Mr. Goodwin, but Jake Layton and I did not kill anyone that we weren't assigned to kill. Every man in that canyon was a Mexican national that day. We were assigned by the Texas Guard. Why would we kill them?"

"I am fully aware for what and by who you were assigned, but we have a credible witness that says otherwise. One of the guardsmen himself who was there. Why would he lie?"

Tuc searched his memory. "Who in the hell...?" He had witnessed every kill that day himself, hadn't he? "Who the hell knows why anyone lies? Usually to save their own hide? Who is your witness?"

Tuc was still baffled. Then he remembered Jake had shot three men, maybe more, down on the canyon floor. Men Tuc never really saw. Why would a Texas guard be among the Mexican rabble that were joining Santa Anna? A turncoat? A paid soldier hired to the highest bidder?

"Sounds pretty thin," Willson finally chimed in.

"Exactly," Tuc agreed.

"Despite your opinions gentlemen, Mr Montgomery's and Mr Layton's arrests are imminent. Unless, that is, you are willing to cooperate with me fully." Henry Wells smiled like he held all the cards and it appeared to Tuc he just might.

The deal had been coerced. The banker and the Texas lawmen made it clear that they meant business. Tucker Montgomery saw little choice, be incarcerated with Jake on the eve of one of the biggest payouts of their lives, or play the game on both sides.

He was a fair card player and understood the importance of the bluff. He would let the lawmen believe he was on their side and agree to give them Jake. He would let Jake believe the same. He would follow Layton's plan as decided, rob the stage and set the blame on the banditos. The only one that would know the whole truth was the smithy driver, Willson.

Tuc would have to trust he was doing the right thing and wait for the situation to present itself that would offer a clearer path. So he made the deal.

Little had Tuc known that Willson was also playing both sides. Jake had brought Willson in on the robbery for extra security, but Scott Willson was an undercover Texas Marshall hired to protect the Wells Fargo cargo from he and Jake. Despite Tuc's arguments against it, Jake had intended to kill the smithy as soon as the robbery was over.

The path got so muddy Tuc didn't know who to trust. Had Layton known about Willson all along? Regardless, Tucker had helped coordinate the death of the lawman. He had somehow misread his long time friend. And now he was party to hunt him down.

Tuc didn't like the game anymore. He felt like he was knee deep in horse shit on this trail. The betrayal stung. He wanted answers from Jake and was determined to get them.

He stood and kicked the dirt over the smoldering embers, spitting on the fire as if to seal the deal in his mind.

He would get answers and get out alive. He wasn't so sure about his friend. The Rangers were on a blood hunt and would certainly kill him, and if Tuc didn't like the answers he got from Jake he might just kill him himself.

He mounted his horse and rode out into the dawn's light alone.

DAWN CAME bright and happy to the narrow desert valley. The sun kissed patches of green grass and roused the birds and insects to a crescendo of morning song. They in turn woke the mining team and their pack animals. Every living thing doing its part to break the day.

Don Juaquin was dressed, packed and ready to move. The anticipation and thrill of the hunt caused a song in his own heart, an intoxication like no other. He was giddy.

He greeted Yesidro jovially, "Señor Don Santiago! What a glorious morning! Are we ready?"

His question made Y feel like a child.

"Of course, Señor," the older man offered. Y's one good eye squinted through a haze of alcohol still lingering from the night before. "We are near, you should have your treasure soon."

Don Juaquin smiled broadly and clapped his hands. "Excellent! Let's move out then shall we?"

He guided Yesidro with his arm around the old man's shoulders toward the horses.

LONG BEFORE DAYBREAK, Jake Layton moved carefully down the canyon on foot and positioned himself where he could watch the mining procession. He felt in his gut that they were not far from their destination. The men had carefully set up tents and corrals the night before with the forethought and precision of a more permanent camp.

He knew enough about mining to know that it would be some time before the actual ore, if found, would make it out of the ground. Something about the way the leader among them moved made Layton believe there was a certainty in this endeavor and it would be worth the wait.

The old man also intrigued him. He seemed to be the key to the whereabouts of whatever it was they were searching for. The leader referred to him often for direction. Jake would keep his eye on the old man.

As if on cue, the two men on Jake's mind rounded the bend and passed just feet below him on the trail. An ancient burro and the dusty crew following faithfully. The old man was a miner, Jake was sure of it. He and his burro were guiding the procession, but whether by free will or force Jake was not certain. Regardless, he could smell advantage over his fellow man and inevitable gain, both of which excited him.

19

———

"Señorita? Señorita?"

It was a whisper, a persistent echo of a man's voice that brought her back to semi-consciousness. Bev's eyelids fluttered, she saw the red skin and blue veins on the inside of the lid but couldn't find the energy to pull them open.

"We must move, Señorita." The voice was clearer and more determined.

A thin boney arm reached around her shoulders and drew her up. She started to resist, but couldn't, though she didn't want to move.

Slowly the unknown, unwanted helper got her feebly on her feet. Head spinning, pain shooting down her shoulder, she thought she would pass out, but somehow she moved with him.

Still blind, her other senses were super sensitized. She felt heat from the small frame beside her, smelled alcohol, dust and manure. Suddenly there was a larger frame in front of her, warm to the touch, hair covered, an animal.

She started at the touch, but was guided carefully to the

boney back of what she realized was a small horse or burro. It was all she could do to maintain her balance as she leaned forward on the beast's neck. The gait, the lulling sounds of the heartbeat and lungs beneath her, and the quiet Spanish words the man was speaking to her and her charge soothed her pain.

Time lapsed. She woke from time-to-time to hear her own groaning and the steady *click click* of hooves on the rock surface below. She felt his hand on the middle of her back for support and then it all slipped away into blackness again.

Images flashed as her mind replayed horrors in her subconscious. Tara in her red car laughing then turning to Bev with no skull and a bloody face. A blood soaked german shepherd lunged out of the darkness and over her head. A cat like woman injected her with a large syringe.

Nothing she could do would stop the reel.

A nude Steve falling in slow motion to the ground. Lights flashing in the darkness and Sam on his knees, hands behind his head execution style. The butt on the rifle smashing her face. She jolted and grabbed the neck of the burro who did not flinch at the movement of his load, instead he plodded patiently onward through the pitch black.

Several times water was carefully introduced to her lips. Then the trek would continue.

The images in her mind slowly began to change, the light behind her eyelids was discernible. There was a steep trail through a dim cave. The neck and ears of a shaggy burro. The happy lolling grin of the same shepherd dog. Sam's face, his eyes lighting up leaning forward to kiss her.

She longed to be with those images, pushing the others back into the darkness. It was an easy choice. Nothing she wanted was in the darkness. She urged herself mentally to the light. She only knew she wanted the light.

With this revelation all motion stopped suddenly. The burro stood quietly, its heart and breathing ceased. The careful warmth of the unknown man's hand on her back was gone. The sound and smell of man and beast were non-existent. Bev felt the momentary panic of a free fall without a net, then the sharp intake of her own breath. She was on solid dry ground. Not falling. Only waking.

She breathed in carefully not opening her eyes, trying to allow her consciousness to catch up to her physical body. She took stock of her now familiar pains.

Her head, her shoulder, her ankles, her hands. All the pieces were there even if not up to their full capabilities. She squeezed her hands open and shut, using her good arm to feel up to the shoulder that was now throbbing. Slowly, very slowly, she opened the one eye that would cooperate.

Her surroundings were blinding. She was outside and it was daylight and warm. That was the extent of what she could discern. She felt no danger, no darkness, so she relaxed and tried to determine what had happened.

20

Yesidro sat on a rock at the edge of the canyon in what little shade the greasewood shrub would allow. He mopped his brow slowly and returned the soiled rag to his shirt pocket. It was cooler in the mine opening but the men stirred up the dust, making the air taste and smell like rock. He took a deep breath and coughed his exhale.

"Not much longer," he spoke to the burro who stood with his head lowered in the same shade swishing his tail at the flies. The burro didn't hear the weight of the comment. Y was sure his death was imminent.

He looked out over the site. Don Juaquin paced at the now yawning mouth in the canyon wall. Y had found the silver door with little trouble, much as he had years ago.

The door itself was a prize find. Thick oak planks banded together with bands of silver and adorned with inlaid precious metal. The fever had struck Don Juaquin in full force when the mine was opened and he sent the men prematurely down into its depth. Unfortunately, the unsecured tunnel had collapsed and the men who had not gone first had spent the last three days digging out their dead companions and supporting the original openings. This was all wearing on the rich man's newly shortened patience.

"What a strange twist of fate," Yesidro pondered.

The silver had been there for at least a couple of hundred years before Y had found it. And sixty plus more since then. Yet the man in charge was having a hard time waiting a few days to get his hands on it. How many men had died in all of that time Yesidro did not know. One would have been too many.

There was a chance that the treasure was gone. Yesidro didn't know how his jefe would respond if that was the case. For now they would both have to wait as the rubble continued to be cleared.

"Not much longer," Yesidro whispered again, rubbing the neck of his trusted friend.

JAKE STRETCHED out under a low growing sage where he could watch the mine activity and doze off if he saw fit. The heat rose out of the canyon and up to the ridge he rested on. A lazy hawk circled overhead searching aimlessly for the movement of a careless rodent on the canyon floor. Nothing moved except the men dragging tarp loads of rubble from the mine entrance and the dust they stirred in the process.

Three days so far.

How long would it take? He had watched the initial scurry of activity at the mine entrance when it first was opened and then collapsed. He had no problem waiting for the hard labor and unknown risks of the treasure's removal to be finished.

The waves of heat and buzz of lazy flies caused Jake's

mind to wander. Strangely, the past came to mind. He wasn't one to dwell on sentiment, but the similarities of the scene below him led his mind back to another canyon and the gunfight between the Mexican freedom fighters and himself so many years ago.

The moment had flashed in his memory before and Jake had determined that it was probably the only mistake he could recall in his career as a gunman. The man in his memory was nondescript. Just another man in the sites of his gun. He was medium height, medium weight and dark haired. He was dressed as a Mexican national, but Jake knew he wasn't a Mexican.

Jake had just shot two Mexicans that had tried to flee the campsite. A slight movement on his right automatically turned his aim and consequent gun fire on the non-Mexican. The man flew back with the concussion of Jake's three bullets. Jake had followed him to where he fell and lay dying.

"Buenos días," Jake greeted him sarcastically grinning, knowing full well the man spoke English. Jake pushed the gun away from the man's body and stooped near the stranger's head. "I believe we may have had a misunderstanding." Jake looked the man in the eye.

"I'm a Texas guard," the man panted.

"How unfortunate."

Jake stood and shot the man in the forehead. Just as he did he heard the clatter of hooves and a zing of a bullet over his ear followed instantly by the gunshot and its echo on the canyon wall. Jake dove for cover and watched another incognito man ride past him and away down the canyon. He had tried to fire, but his gun was empty.

"Damn." A loose end that he was sure would haunt him one day.

This single thought was the only thing that disturbed his calloused mind. The unconscious concern interrupted his nap...or maybe the hawk was screeching. Jake started from sleep.

There was extra movement and noise coming from the mine. Men excitedly came in and out of the opening with new energy like ants that had been disturbed.

He couldn't make out the words they were saying, but something had changed. The man in charge grabbed what the men from the mine were hauling out.

He held it up, turning it in his hand. The object gleamed in the dusty late afternoon light. The man in charge grinned, throwing his head back and laughing silently.

Jake grinned, too. "Time to move."

21

———

Bev tried to unravel the reality of the last few days from the images of her subconscious mind. The line between the two was still blurry.

She was still alive. She knew that.

She could feel the sun on her skin, the beat of her heart and the wince of pain from various parts of her body. She breathed slowly and deeply letting oxygen clear her foggy brain.

How many days ago had it been that she was laying in the sun, nude, whole and not afraid? She couldn't remember. Then the hike, the gun fire, and Tara and Steve were dead.

She had found Sam and B, or they had found her. The hike through the desert and the ambush of the drug lord and his daughter. The gun fight and her last conscious recollection of being slammed with the butt of a large gun. Then hanging in the cave and falling, and then the ride out of the cave.

She sighed deeply. Reaching up, she touched the gash

above her eye. It was crusted over and tender. Where was Sam? Was he still alive?

Her running thoughts suddenly stopped.

A man and a burro had given her a ride. An all too familiar auto response of fear rose up in her. Where were they? Who was he?

She opened her good eye fully and raised up.

Would they be back? Her fear gave way to wonder. She didn't sense the old man was a threat, wherever he was. She looked at her surroundings, having to hold her hand over her good eye to shade the glare.

She seemed to be alone along a canyon wall of a fairly wide arroyo. It still looked like Arizona high desert, cactus, scrub brush, bleached sandy terrain.

She pulled herself up against the rock wall. Every effort was exhausting and she had to immediately lay her head back.

"How in the hell..." she wondered out loud trying to surmise how she had gotten from the bottom of the cave to the bottom of the canyon.

Her stomach growled loudly in response. She was starving and extremely thirsty. She couldn't wait to find out about her mystery aide or for him to reappear. Not too far off in the distance were some cottonwood trees. There had to be water.

Suddenly how she got there didn't matter. All that mattered was abating her thirst and staying alive.

She looked at her legs. Her ankles were cut and swollen and she was barefoot. She bent up one scuffed knee then the other. Nothing seemed out of joint or broken.

Thank God for small favors, she thought.

As she rolled onto her good shoulder side she was pleased to find that her rib cage was no longer sore.

"Two small favors!" she exclaimed as she pushed herself up on one hand and her knees, then up to kneeling.

Her head spun from the pain in her injured shoulder and more than likely a concussion from the fall in the cave. She was going to have to get her arm in a sling. She felt her pockets, knowing full well that the knife had most likely fallen into the depths of the cave, and was proven correct. Luckily the men's T-shirt she was wearing was already ripped in a couple places. She had seen someone make a sling from a T-shirt somewhere before, maybe Girl Scouts.

Basically one handed and on her knees, she proceeded to rip a vertical strip under her good arm. After a couple attempts she brought it around her back and used her teeth and good hand to tie it to the bottom corner of the front of the torn shirt around her injured arm. This was not without cursing, guttural growls of pain and war cries of frustration.

"Shit!" She panted from exertion when the knot was finally tightened, beads of sweat on her forehead and chest, eyes tearing from the pain.

Her arm was secure. She caught her breath and slowly stood up, using the rock wall for balance then took another moment, just leaning. Suddenly the thought of what she must look like crossed her mind and she laughed out loud. The sound echoed off the canyon wall.

"Like something from Walking Dead," Bev joked to herself.

Putting her full weight on her legs she felt no sharp pain. Another good sign. No broken bones or nothing out of joint, but the bare feet were going to be a problem.

She peered into the distance at the trees again and the ground below. Gravel, hot sand and every thorny plant known to man lay between her and her goal. She set her sights, grabbed a sturdy stick to walk with and began making her way gingerly across the valley floor.

22

———

Long deepening evening shadows made it easy for Jake to maneuver off the rim of the canyon and ever closer to the mine. The men had continued to bring what he was certain was silver from the mouth of the cave for most of the afternoon. The haul looked large even from this distance and excited him, driving him closer.

It was just beginning to grow dark and the men of the camp were lighting lanterns when Jake posted himself at the edge of the mine. He could hear most of what was being said and understood enough of the Spanish to confirm that his thoughts were correct. A large silver treasure had been found deep in the mine.

"Date prisa!" Don Juaquin implored the last man out of the mine. His patience ever waning even with the treasure at his feet. He straddled the pile on the tarp like a conquistador.

"Cuánto más?" he asked the worker.

"Necesitamos uno día más, Señor." The man stated, wiping his forehead on his sleeve. "Es un largo camino abajo."

"Bien," Juaquin finally dismissed the man who gratefully ambled towards camp, leaving him alone with his silver.

Jake watched the man ponder the treasure.

Juaquin bent down and picked up a rudimentary coin, turning it over in his hand. The pile consisted of many of these and other silver objects as well as some ore with veins of the blue silver running through them. Jake had never seen such a thing. Suddenly Don Juaquin looked up, straight into the darkness where Jake stood.

Jake's hand moved silently to the gun at his side. Juaquin's stare lasted a long moment until a grin grew slowly across his lips.

Not a grin born out of joy, but one of evil. Even Jake's hair on the back of his neck stood up.

Juaquin stood and spun around and Jake eased his thumb off the hammer of the gun. The man wasn't looking at him after all, just through him.

"Don Yesidro!" Juaquin shouted down the path towards the canyon camp, striding that way and out of site. He was gone long enough that Jake was tempted to jump into the lamplight and fill his saddle bag when he heard the two men coming back up the path followed by the burro.

Don Juaquin's arm was draped around the frail old man's shoulders in an act of what Jake was sure was false brotherhood. He spoke loudly to the old man as if he couldn't hear.

"Mi Amigo! We have done it!" Juaquin pulled the old man to him, shaking him in celebration.

"Si, it would seem so Señor," Y replied. "Just as I said." The burro blew his nose loudly behind them as if in agreement.

"We shall be rich men. You have done well."

Don Juaquin left Y's side and went to the pile in the lamplight. He held up two handfuls of valuables and let them drop ceremoniously back onto the pile with a clatter. The same strange look Jake had seen earlier crossed his face.

"Or I will," Juaquin murmured, unheard by the old man. He turned to face the weathered one-eyed guide and his burro, drawing his pistol from his waistband.

Y didn't look shocked, but he did put himself between his jefe and his burro, carefully backing the burro to the cave opening. Jake squinted at the scene.

"You see old man, this is a lot of money. There's plenty to share for sure, but, well…I don't share well."

He moved slowly towards Yesidro and the burro. The old man's face didn't change. He didn't beg, he didn't look alarmed or afraid.

"Si Señor. I knew that," he finally said.

Don Juaquin cocked his head, slightly amused, taking a moment to respond.

"Then you will understand what I must do."

He grinned and leveled his arm to take aim. Jake made his move and stepped into the light just slightly behind the younger man.

"No esta noche, Señor."

Jake's words startled Don Juaquin for just a moment before he turned to take aim at the surprise intruder. But Jake had a moment's head start and struck Juaquin across the temple with the handle of his gun sending him reeling, scattering the pile of treasure.

Jake followed quickly, jumping on and pinning the stunned man to the ground with a knee on his neck. Juaquin spit Spanish curse words and struggled under the weight of the other man, hitting and kicking, but Jake had him overpowered. Yesidro and the burro retreated into the mouth of the cave.

"It's too bad, Señor," Jake hissed at the man below him. "That you will never see the reward of all the work you have had others do for you." Jake thrust his knee farther into Juaquin's throat.

Juaquin's eyes went black with hate and he flailed with one last exerted effort. Jake chuckled, pressing his knee deeper. He watched the look in Don Juaquin's eyes change from rage to sudden fear and at last panic before his life extinguished. Jake was glad he didn't have to shoot and alert the camp, but it wouldn't be long before someone came looking. He released his hold, rolled the body aside and began packing the treasure.

He filled bags as full as he could carry and turned to take the load to his horse, which he had left down the canyon. That's when he heard a shuffle from the mine opening.

Jake paused and set the bags down. He waved the old man to him, but Yesidro didn't move. Jake closed the distance instead, stepping towards them.

"There's a lot of treasure old man," Jake said.

Yesidro fixed his seeing eye on Jake and said nothing.

"Too much to carry in one load, I'll have to come back." Jake stopped just within reach looking into the leathery face of Y.

"Or.." Jake grabbed the lead of the burro and pulled the beast to him with some resistance. It was the only time the old man started to move or protest.

"Ah-ah-ah," Jake waved the gun and Yesidro released his hold on his friend.

The burro took a few steps forward before realizing he

was under the lead of a stranger and then halted, not to be moved. No amount of pushing, pulling or swatting would make the beast budge an inch.

"He will not go without me," was Yesidro's only advice.

Jake met the old man's stare and let the burro's lead drop. The animal stepped back, stopping at the side of his longtime companion.

"So be it," Jake rushed them with sudden rage, pushing them both back inside the cave.

There was a lantern casting futile light into the pitch black that yawned beyond. At the edge of the light's glow was an obvious drop and the burro skidded to the edge and stopped, sensing danger.

Jake unceremoniously drew his gun and shot the animal through the skull, watching the horror on the old man's face as the animal fell to its front knees and tumbled into the blackness below in what seemed like slow motion.

Yesidro had seconds to turn and see the face of his attacker in the flash of the second shot. It was the look he had seen before on Don Juaquin's face, evil, obsessed, uncontrolled, as if the two men had exchanged spirits.

Jake Layton's bullet hit his second mark and Don Yesidro Santiago's earthly conscious existence switched to black as quickly as a candle extinguished in a mine and as dark as the hole into which his frail tired body fell.

Jake strode the two steps to the edge of the abyss and spit into the blackness after the two.

"No mistakes, no loose ends," he stated. Then he turned, walked out of the mine and gathered all the silver he could carry to his mount.

Tuc Montgomery waited a moment just outside the lamplight's reach into the shadows beyond the mine entrance. He had patiently watched and heard the entire exchange. Silently, Tuc's blood ran cold and he moved to follow a man he no longer recognized.

23

Water. Who would imagine the simplest most basic of elements, such a common daily part in every life of human, plant and animal, could become such a pure indulgent luxury, so desired, so intoxicating, so quenching.

Bev lay in the cool spring, floating just beneath the surface, immersed in liquid healing.

The water lapped at her wounds and cooled the skin on her bruised arms, legs and feet. She had crawled the last fifty feet across the sandy canyon floor.

She smelled the pool long before it came into her view. Driven like an animal at the end, she fell head long into the cattails and drank her fill. The hollow sound of the water in her ears echoed deep in her head and for a moment the whole world faded away, she simply floated.

Water had always been her go to. As a young girl she swam on teams, finding the rhythmic sound of water rushing through her ears peaceful. She had absorbed the energy of rain on rooftops and tree leaves, or babbling over smooth stones, or lapping upon white sandy beaches. As an adult she had sought those same comforts on vacations and retreats to tropical islands and cool rainy mountaintops. She thought she could never love water more, until now.

Bev lay still. Letting the water lift and sustain her rehydration.

She could hear her heart beat and the lapping of water surrounding her. Tears welled up under her closed eyelids. She had lost the ability to cry for the past few days due to dehydration. No more. She let the tears stream down her face uninterrupted and back into the pool around her, silently at first and then accompanied by a low moan. She sobbed, as much from gratitude to be alive as from exhaustion and pain in body and spirit.

The mix of emotions surfaced from inside her and released into a wail, until they were extinguished and she continued to float...empty.

She wondered if she could sleep floating here on a pool of tears. Just float and it would all be better. Let the water take her down and put her to sleep.

She began to drift off the bank to the deeper end of the pool and a darker part of her heart and mind. She understood why people might give up, when their spirit couldn't take another moment of grief or pain. She could let the water swallow it all, all that she contained, tears, grief, pain, exhaustion. Just swallow her whole. Like Ophelia in Hamlet, *"....like a creature native and endued unto that element...to a muddy death"*.

The water rocked and suddenly pitched Bev over, pushed by some sudden movement from the shore. She was caught up in splashing waves and swam instinctively. Her eyes flew open to the bounding wet shaggy creature before her. In a flash of lolling licks and happy barking, Bev was jolted back to inexplicable joy as the familiar frame of B floundered against her in the water.

"Oh my God! B!" she sputtered and kissed the end of the long snout.

She had never been so happy to see another living creature. B returned her kisses and licked her face, whining the same emotions.

"Where have you been? Good girl!"

The dog spun and rolled accepting Bev's hugs and rubs. She was thin, but looked okay. Finally B lay down beside Bev in the pool, intermittently panting, drinking and checking Bev with her snout to stroke her head.

"It's okay. Good girl. It's going to be okay," as Bev said it, she somehow honestly believed and so did the dog. They sat in the cool water, leaning on each other, just taking a moment to reassure their belief.

The dog didn't stay still long. She jumped back to the edge of the water, spun around and began barking incessantly. Childhood scenes from the TV show Lassie came to Bev's mind. Nothing would surprise her now.

"What is it girl?" Bev questioned the dog.

B continued to bark, obviously wanting Bev to do something.

"Okay, okay, let me get up."

The shepherd lunged back in the water then back to the edge of the pool, excited to get a reaction. She continued to bark as Bev got upright, secured her t-shirt sling and found a stick to lean on.

"Lead the way!" Bev finally said and B shot off down river. "Slowly!" Bev shouted, grinning. "Unbelievable," she muttered and hobbled off after the dog.

B stuck to the edge of the small creek bed, instinctively knowing the muddy ground was easier on both of their feet and keeping the water source close. It was slow going and the dog would pause to allow Bev to catch up and rest, then continue on, much like she had in the desert days ago when they had first met. Steadily they made their way.

After a while, Bev guessed not more than a mile, B took a well beaten trail away from the creek and up towards the side of the canyon, then stopped at a widened spot in the trail that looked to be a dead end. When Bev stopped and looked around, B started barking at the wall of the canyon that at first glance looked like a solid rock covered with brush. Bev moved closer.

"What is it?" Bev was beginning to wonder if the Lassie thing was such a great idea. B began to dig at the base of the scrub. "Get back, B," Bev commanded, but the dog wouldn't be called off. Dirt was flying from between her legs. "B! Back!" Bev tried her best impersonation of Sam's commands to control the dog. "Sit!"

B hesitated, backed up and sat down, panting and whining madly.

"Stay," Bev bent over and looked under the shrub. At first all she could see was the rock wall. She moved the dirt at the bottom where B had been working. There, covered in sand and time, was what appeared to be an old wooden door. It was in the rock wall, hidden from view by the overgrowth. The dog had cleared almost all of the casing.

"What the heck?" Bev sat back and watched the obsessed dog.

Suddenly B stopped her panting and cocked her head looking past Bev to the door. Bev paused as well. They waited. The dog seemed to hold her breath. So did Bev. There were the distant sounds of buzzing flies and a light breeze through shrubs but nothing else.

Then she heard it. A low sound, an unusual sound for

the canyon around them, an echoing groan coming from behind the rock wall, a man's groan deep behind the door.

B barked and jumped back to her task pawing feverishly at the ground. Bev put her bad shoulder against the dog and joined in with all of her might. Sam was alive and behind that door.

24

Father Miguel counted the toll of the last evening bell under his breath. It was his habit, an end of day ritual that brought another day of service to the Lord to a close.

"Nueve.....diez....." he whispered to himself as he walked the path at the perimeter of the chapel, the moonlight leading the way.

He knew the path by heart and didn't need the cool silver light to guide him. He padded softly with his tired eyes half closed, hands tucked in his robes anticipating the rest that awaited him as he had many times before. The grounds were still and peaceful.

He heard the quick movement in the dark, but never saw who administered the blow that sent him reeling off the path, unconscious. The Father's robes twirled around his body as he rolled slowly down an embankment, coming to rest with a soft unnatural sound.

Jake Layton turned his rifle in his hand from using it like a club and watched the body settle. When he was satisfied that the priest wasn't getting up he strode towards the dim light of the sanctuary. If there was anything valuable in this place it would be there.

It had taken everything in Juan Carlos's power not to cry out as he watched the scene unfold from behind the wall of the church cemetery. He had gone there as he did every night to pray at his father's grave. Instead, he held his breath and watched the armed man strike his beloved priest from behind with the butt of the rifle. He watched in horror as Father Miguel wilted and rolled away down the slope like a discarded stone. As soon as the man left he jumped to his benefactor's aid.

Juan slid down the slope and fell on his knees beside the priest. Juan could see the damage to the back of Father Miguel's skull, the moonlight glistened on the pulsing blood, highlighting the exposed white bone. Juan wept and prayed as he turned the large man to his back.

"Please God, do not leave me. Please God, do not leave him." His prayer fervent even in a tortured whisper.

Father Miguel lifted his hand to the boy's face, but did not open his eyes. Juan Carlos pressed his forehead and cheek hard into the comfort of the gesture. The Father was breathing in heavy uneven breaths, the boy pressed his head to the Father's chest.

"Juan," Father finally said softly. "Juan, it's going to be all right...you must get help."

The boy shook his head violently in protest, holding tight.

Father Miguel patted Jaun's cheek where his hand rested. "You must get help."

"I don't want you to leave me, Father," the boy choked through his tears. "I won't leave you."

"I will not leave you and God will not leave you. We will always be with you. The boys will need your help. I need you to get them help. God will be with you," Father Miguel spoke sternly but softly. "Go to the priest's quarters and find Father James." Father Miguel slowly placed his hand on Juan's shoulder encouraging him to go. "Do not be afraid. Go. God will help you."

Juan stood and wiped his bleary eyes and runny nose with the back of his hand, then took the priest's hand in his and kissed it. "I love you Father." With that the boy bolted down the dim path.

"And I you, my Son. It will be all right." Tears welled in the cleric's eyes and for a split second the love of this world tugged at his penitent heart. "Be with him, Lord. Protect them, Lord," he whispered into the night.

He moved the rosary painstakingly to his lips and began the recitation that he had memorized from childhood, the repetition always a comfort. His breathing evened. He saw his failures and shortcomings dismissed, he felt his defiance and selfishness forgiven, his worthlessness made suddenly worthy. Not once did he regret his life of devotion.

He breathed in one last deep breath of the night air and peace flooded over him. A peace he had never known. He felt the words resound in his head and his heart, "Well done my good and faithful servant." Pastor Miguel suddenly and softly slept with every saint, sinner, King and pauper before him that believed, and his rest was complete.

<hr>

JUAN RACED down the footpath that led to the back of a long low building behind the main sanctuary to find Father James. The tears had dried and his jaw was set in sheer determination. It was darker in the shrubbery between the buildings and in his haste Juan did not see the man until he was right in front of him. Juan ran right into the stranger's waist, startling them both. Strong hands grabbed the boy's shoulders and then covered his mouth.

"Be quiet boy," the man whispered. "Silencio," he added.

Juan did not flinch, only tried to breathe heavily through the hand over his face. At first he thought it was the man he had just seen with Father Miguel, but as he caught his breath and focused he realized this man was much bigger with a different hat.

Juan was more afraid than ever. There were two banditos. Fear rose in the boy's belly. He had failed. They would kill them all he was certain.

As if understanding the boys thoughts the man stated, "I won't hurt you boy, do you understand? Comprende?"

Juan nodded.

The man kept his hand in place, bent down to the boy's level, gazed directly into his eyes and continued in a whisper, "I am hunting the man that just killed the Padre."

"Killed?" Juan's heart sunk, the Father was dead. Tears welled in his eyes and he panted for air.

"Did you see which way the man went?"

The man's hat was tipped back and Juan could see his eyes. They were earnest and stern and Juan wanted to trust him. He nodded. The man uncovered the boy's mouth, but kept his grip on his arm.

"Where?"

Juan pointed to the sanctuary behind them standing dark and quiet, the moon lighting up its smooth white stucco sides and glinting on the stained glass. Both the boy and the man saw a flicker of light from within the building.

The big man stood and, without losing sight of the light in the window, he directed the boy, "Run and get the others to safety boy. I will take care of this."

Juan saw the star on the big man's chest, a lawman.

"Si, Señor." Juan paused for a moment to watch the man head away into the shadows. "Gracias Dios," he muttered and crossed himself then continued on his path to warn the others.

25

─────

Between the two good paws of the dog and Bev's one good arm it wasn't long before the base of the doorway was cleared away. Bev followed the worn edge around, clearing the overgrowth away from the sides and top as well, exposing an obvious entrance in the side of the hill with rock all around. Maybe an old mine.

The door was mostly wood, but was girded with metal bands and hardware that had tarnished black with time. She pushed and pulled it with no result. Extremely heavy, it was set in place.

"There has to be a way," she thought out loud, searching the area for something, anything, she could use as leverage. She doubted the dry shrubbery in the arroyo would be sturdy enough. They would have to break through.

B paced at Bev's heals as she looked around the area for some rocks. If they got too far from the door, the dog would return, not wanting to leave her post.

After some searching Bev came up with a stone that she could hold and another that was sharp at one end. Hopefully they would work as blunt force. She did not know how she was going to hold them both at the same time, but she had to try.

"Ready?" she asked the ever impatient shepherd.

Bev used her knee to steady the pointed rock as she held it with her bad arm. Then, with a sideways swing, she struck the blunt stone to the other.

She cried out. "Shit!" The pain reverberated up through her arm and into her shoulder, but there was a dent in the wood. B spun around barking, encouraging her to suck it up.

Bev grit her teeth, held her breath and struck again. The wood splintered, but did not give way.

"One more," she panted.

Pulling back further and striking her target, the sharp stone shot out of her hand and through the antique wood leaving a fist sized hole. B stuck her nose through sniffing madly, then whining and biting at the door.

"Let me see." Bev pushed the dog aside and used the rock still in her hand to continue to widen the hole.

As the structure's integrity weakened, it began to come apart in larger pieces. Before Bev could stop her, B squeezed through the opening into the pitch black beyond.

"B! No! Come!" Bev was on her stomach peering through the opening. "B!" She could hear the dog a ways away and the familiar moan. "Oh, God! Sam?!" Bev screamed into the dark.

With strength that surprised her, she broke away the bottom of the door and crawled through. The smell was sickeningly familiar. Dark, damp, bloody. It was like replaying a nightmare that she couldn't wake up from.

"Sam? B?"

She felt blindly, then the light from the hole in the door began to penetrate and her eyes adjusted. She could see his dark frame leaned up against a less dark wall and the flash of the dog's wet nose and eyes. Carefully, she crawled to them, feeling her way.

B wagged her tail and greeted her for a moment then went back to Sam's side, as if to say, "See, here he is!"

"Good girl B," Bev praised.

She carefully pulled herself up next to Sam, gently feeling for his breathing and heartbeat. Both present, but weak.

She blindly felt over the rest of his body. He had a head injury at the base of his skull, a large lump but no blood. His face was swollen on one side and crusted from the ear, nose, eye and mouth. He moaned when she reached his shoulder which seemed distended and out of the socket. She smelled blood and his shirt was stiff. She could not tell where the wound was, but he had lost significant blood.

Suddenly, his hand reached up and grabbed her forearm.

"AAAAAUUM!"

It was a sound an animal would make not a man. Bev and B both jumped, startled by the volume reverberating in the cavern around them.

"Sam," Bev said directly. "It's me, Bev. B is with me. We're going to help you."

Sam's heart suddenly beat wildly and he panted, letting her go. She had to get him water and some sort of light in here.

"Stay B." She knew she didn't have to say it, the dog wasn't going anywhere. Bev scooted back to the opening in the door and crawled into the blinding light of day.

"If I make it out of this alive," Bev spoke to herself as she worked. "I am never going camping again."

How long had it been since she had eaten anything? Days? She was working on starting a fire through friction. It was something she had seen in a movie and doubted it really would work. Bending over the wooden trough she had fashioned with the tinder in place, she worked the stick in her hand to create heat. Time after time. Nothing.

She stopped.

"Please, God."

It was an honest petition to a higher power she wasn't sure existed, but she had come to the end of her own thoughts and strength and had nowhere else to turn.

"Please," she whispered earnestly.

She did not want to die this way, she didn't want Sam to die either. Taking a deep breath she started again. Steadily she worked and thought with a glimmer of hope that she could feel the heat increasing. Then, finally, a thin tail of smoke curled up from the tinder.

"Oh my God! Oh my God!"

She carefully blew and the ember blazed.

"Thank you, thank you," she said with relief.

Bev scrambled for more tinder and built a small fire. There was hope.

She brought cattails from the stream and chopped off their root with her handy rock. They could be eaten, she thought. Piece by piece she took the fire, more wood for fuel and the meager meal into the cave. On her last trip she soaked her shirt in the stream and used it like a sponge to slowly drip water into Sam's mouth.

His wounds were finally visible in the firelight. A dislocated shoulder, much like her own, maybe worse. Several blows to the head and face and a gunshot wound in his mid-side that had gone all the way through. It was packed with mud, front and back, something Sam must have done to stop the bleeding.

Other than scrapes and bruises, the rest of him looked to be okay. As he took in more water, his blood pressure and breathing became stronger. She didn't move him or touch any of the injuries so as not to poke the sleeping bear.

Drawing from some unknown inner strength that pushed her onward, Bev was tireless. She fed the fire and kept ministering the water. They were going to make it. She and the dog placed themselves on either side of him to keep him warm and tried to rest.

Thank God. They were going to make it.

26

———

The lawman peered into a low lying stained glass window from his hidden vantage point at the back of the building. Candlelight flickered through the colored glass as Jake found his way through the sanctuary. He was at the front of the room and a series of clatters gave Tuc the impression that Jake was ransacking the church.

"What the hell?' Tuc whispered to himself, wondering what was driving his lifelong friend and brother to this madness.

Ever since the thought of the stage robbery plan had been hatched, a part of Jake's personality emerged, a part that Tuc had never seen.

He had personally witnessed Jake kill four innocent people in cold blood, the woman at the stage stop, the Marshall Scott Willson, the old Miner and just a few minutes ago, a priest. It wasn't hard to believe that he had also killed the other man in the canyon and who knew how many others. Tuc could not understand why, but it was clear Jake was not the man Tuc had once known. He had to be stopped.

Tuc Montgomery stood quietly to his full height and silently removed the pistol from his side holster. He drew a long deep breath and with stealth that belied his stature, he turned into the open back door of the church.

Tuc had been in a few churches in his life, but the beauty of the sanctuary even dimly lit by the thief's candle, gave him momentary pause.

Silver gilding glinted on every carved surface, inlaid in every piece of furniture and floor tile. Windows ran down both sides of the room and each window sill held a candelabra of ornate Spanish design with multiple arms all made of silver. At the front of the church the altar gleamed in a deep blue iridescent silver, completely overlaid in the precious metal. Even the cross and the Crucified Christ which hung there were gilded with silver designs. It took the big man's breath away.

His awe was interrupted by a deep chuckle from behind the altar.

"Pretty impressive, huh?" Jake indicated with a sweep of his arm at the glory that surrounded them.

His face was partially lit by the candle nearby casting an eerie shadow on his crooked smile. He quickly went back to the pile of silver church articles that he was packing as if there was nothing out of the ordinary.

"How'd you find me, T?" Jake asked, bent over his work. He didn't wait for an answer, but rather spoke fast and moved faster. "I didn't expect to see you for several months, you know, until we all got back to Texas. You know, your ranch, your homestead, a wife. Wasn't that the plan? What happened to the plan? How long have you been looking for me?"

Suddenly Jake swung around, weapon drawn.

His speech slowed, "I guess the real question is why were you looking?" He cocked the pistol and took aim.

Tuc jumped behind a pillar at his side, hearing the ping of the bullet ricochet off into the dark.

"Jake!" Tuc was stilled stunned by the man's behavior. "What is going on?"

"Going on?" Jake paused with a mocking look of deep thought. "Well, I'm taking stock of my spiritual life, so to speak. What's going on with you?" He laughed at his own joke.

"You don't need this stuff. We got plenty from the stage." Tuc tried to reason with him as he moved closer in the shadows. "C'mon, let's get out of here. Stealing from the church... it just ain't right."

The lawman attempted to sound sincere while at the same time trying to determine where exactly Jake's gun was aimed. The dim light made it difficult.

Jake snorted. Unimpressed with Tuc's spiritual reasoning.

"They can get more. There's a mine full of it in the mountain. I thought about mining it myself but this seems easier." He paused, listening in the dark. "Tuc, I need to know. Are you for me or against me?" Jake waited.

Tuc thought about it.

"Keep in mind, we're in church," Jake quipped.

"Jake. I've been looking for you. There are some questions about the job we did in the canyon for the Texas guard."

Tuc watched Jake's reaction. For a moment he stopped and cocked his head slightly and for that moment Tuc spied the recognizable face of his friend.

Jake shook his head in disgust. "Damn, loose ends," he mumbled.

Hoping to sway Jake into peaceably coming with him, Tuc continued, "They sent me to find you so we could clear it up."

"They? Who the hell are 'They'?" Jake started to move off the altar and towards Tuc.

"What the hell difference does that make?" Tuc could feel sweat trickle down the center of his back. Jake was losing patience.

Tucker moved into the open to face him. Jake stopped, caught off guard not only at the reminder of the size of the man, but of a sentimentality he didn't expect to feel. His childhood friend, the man who had shared his life, saved his life, something started to shift in his mind and almost his heart. Then the moonlight caught a glint on the big man's chest and Jake saw the star.

Even in the gun smoke shadowed light, Tuc saw Jake's face and eyes turn to steel.

"You killed Willson...he was a Texas–" Tuc began, but before he could finish the sentence Jake fired.

"Against me," Jake stated as he fired off two more rounds, backing up.

Tuc returned fire and dove to the floor between the pews. He watched Jake's shadow move to the front corner of the room and disappear.

Tuc followed him quickly through a doorway, the one that led up the staircase of the church bell tower.

27

The constant hot breath of an unseen monster blew from one direction, then the opposite. Bev could never get a fix on its location. She knew it was sinister without ever seeing its form. It taunted and twisted her like a bug caught in a web. The feeling of helplessness and impotence against her attacker was terrifying.

A tiny spark of light flashed and lit the pitch darkness. It flickered and moved with the air current. Bev twisted and searched in the dim illumination, but there was still no sign of her adversary. The spark grew quickly into a consuming blaze. She struggled to leave, but couldn't.

The fire crossed the floor beneath her and created a pitch black smoke that curled slowly up her legs and up around her shoulders. It was heavy, thick and greasy. She couldn't move from underneath its weight. It had a presence, a chilling agenda. The smoke thickened and twisted around her middle, up her torso, squeezing her lungs and moving to her neck.

She panted desperately. She was being suffocated once again, drowning in its filthy mass. Heat rose from below. As before, she tried to struggle, but didn't have the strength. Tried to scream, but didn't have the air. Tried to cry, but didn't have the tears. She didn't want to, but she felt herself giving in, she was so tired.

The smoke knew her weakness and shuddered with anticipation, quickening its movements. The blackness beckoned. So appealing. Everything was so still, so calm, at last she could rest. Just rest.

"Just rest," a voice commanded in her mind, with an assurance and love that Bev had never heard before. She turned away from the cold stillness of the dark, longing to see the source of these feelings, of the peace that suddenly enveloped her.

The light was bright and warm, not burning like the fire, and its gentle presence somehow refueled and refreshed her. The darkness recoiled, not able to stay in the presence of the light, and the smoke suddenly cleared. Fear was gone. Clarity filled the space and there was only peace.

Bev took a deep clean breath and felt rested and renewed. A stirring at her side caused her eyelids to flutter open.

A dream, she thought. Somehow as she came into consciousness she knew that she would never have that dark dream again. The peace and light that had abated her enemy was in her spirit.

"Thank you, God," she whispered and felt the man next to her breathing and the dog beside him move in the dark.

Her eyes welled with tears, she was so grateful to be alive no matter what condition. So grateful that she wasn't alone.

"God, please get us out of this. Give me strength. Please don't let anything happen to Sam."

Her tears were hot, sincere. B sensed her emotion and whimpered from where she lay guard. Bev put her arm across Sam and her hand on the dog's head, letting the tears stream.

No one could have convinced her that she would ever feel this way. That she would care about someone like this, love someone like this. It was a different level of love that she was unfamiliar with, a pure desire for the ultimate good of someone else with no regard for what she would receive. Unconditional love.

Had she always been such a hard case? Did it really take this kind of trauma to move her to this realization? Had she been so self-centered all her life?

The only answer resounding in her head was a definite 'Yes'.

"Forgive me, Lord," she whispered, recognizing the missing piece of the puzzle in her life.

Suddenly the dog started, ears alert, a familiar low growl rising from her chest.

Bev jolted out of her thoughts and went on full alert, signaling the dog with the pressure of her hand to be still. In the dark, her hearing was almost as heightened as B's. She heard it, too. Not the flutter of bats, the trickle of distant water or the shift of stones in the cave that she had already become accustomed to, this noise came from outside.

Footsteps.

There was someone outside the door of the mine.

28

———

Jake had the advantage, the high ground. The stairs wound up in a spiral, the only light cast by the moon through occasional small windows. Tuc could see Jake's shadow appear on the curved white walls as he moved quickly upward.

The air was heavy in the stairway and sweat ran into the big man's eyes, behind his ears and down his neck. His large frame filled the stairway and was an easy target at every turn.

"Damn," he cussed the whole event. Mopping his brow he continued his pursuit, climbing the three stories cautiously, listening for any change in Jake's clamor, not knowing when the staircase ended or where it would ultimately lead.

Suddenly, the racing footsteps on the stairs ahead of him stopped. Tuc drew back.

Jake cocked his gun and fired down the stairwell. The bullet ricocheted off the stucco and whizzed past Tucker's ear. He pulled up against the wall as best he could. He was fairly certain it was a blind shot. If he couldn't see Jake, Jake couldn't see him.

Tuc crouched to his belly and crawled as low as possible, slowly, quietly, keeping to the dark floor, listening.

As he moved upward the air got cooler. Wherever the stairs led it was open to the outdoors somehow. His eyes were adjusting to the darkness and he saw faint light ahead. Jake would be waiting to shoot him. He paused and listened again, silence. Jake was listening, too.

Tuc took off his hat, mopping the sweat from his face once more. Carefully, with one motion, he pulled his feet under him and tossed the hat out into the space in front of him. Jake's gunfire filled the air with sound and flashes of light as he unloaded shot after shot at the decoy. Tuc leaped in the opposite direction of the flying hat hoping to find some sort of cover.

He bounded out onto a wooden platform surrounded by large open windows set in white stucco walls. It only took seconds for Jake to identify his real target and Tuc could feel the rain of bullets in the air around him and the sound of chimes as they missed him and struck something resonate in the center of the room.

A bell. They were in the top of bell tower.

The silver bell hung halfway down from the ceiling in the center of the room. It was suspended over an opening in the floor by a tangle of ropes which hung through to the ringing room below.

Instinctively, Tuc tried to keep the bell between himself and his attacker. He felt a familiar burning in his upper left arm and knew he had been hit. Warm blood soaked his shirt. With the deep growl of a caged animal, Tucker Montgomery turned and faced Jake.

Jake was stoic, unmoved, determined. Tuc knew at that

moment Jake was going to kill him. The muzzle of the pistol flashed and in slow motion Tuc went down, stumbling forward to his knees at the edge of the opening in the floor. The bullet had hit somewhere in his midsection taking the wind out of him, but he wasn't dead yet.

Jake rushed him and Tucker threw all his weight at him, slamming him to the floor. Floor boards shook, even the bell swung slightly with the heavy concussion. Both men fighting their enemy, fighting for their lives.

They pitched to the outer edge of the room, Tuc half stumbling but still outweighing and overpowering his opponent. Tuc pinned Jake with his forearm against the white stucco window ledge, pushing him, intending to send him over the edge into the night below.

Jake's gun went off again ripping through Tuc's left shoulder, sending him reeling back on the floor. The blood loss and pain immobilized the big man.

Jake stood up slowly, kicking Tuc's gun across the room. Moving with calculated indifference he reloaded his gun as he walked to Tucker's side.

Tucker's left arm hung limply through the opening under the bell. Jake placed his boot on Tucker's right shoulder, putting his weight into it. Tucker groaned, his heart pounding throughout his body like a helpless rabbit. He turned to look Jake in the eye.

"What went wrong?" he asked breathlessly. He searched for an answer in Jake's eyes that he knew wouldn't be there.

Jake smiled. "I think everything went just right." Then he cocked the gun and aimed at the center of Tucker's forehead.

Time stood still for one unearthly moment, no sound, no movement, no thought.

There was a bang and a loud hiss. It took an instant for

Tucker to realize that the sound hadn't come from the gun. Jake was still smiling, but there was movement from above him, a whirling sound getting faster and faster that finally drew Jake's attention upward as well.

Tucker saw the bell pitch just as the beam that it was suspended on gave way with a loud crack. Tucker rolled towards Jake's feet and in a whip of ropes the bell came crashing from the ceiling, catching Jake's shoulder and plunging through the floor, taking Jake with it in a cloud of clanging smoke and shower of splintering wood.

Tucker stayed curled on the floor holding his ears at the sound, waiting. Part of him was waiting for Jake to take his last shot and part of him knew decidedly that he was gone.

When the ringing in his head finally stopped, Tucker drew himself up to his knees and used his good arm to crawl slowly to the center of the room.

The scene below was one he would never forget the rest of his life. The ringing room was lit by the moon, settling dust dancing through the beams of light. There were piles of misplaced rope cast from corner to corner, and in the center was Jake's lifeless body, clinging to the huge silver bell that crushed his chest. The look on Jake's face was not terror or pain, but as if he was pleased with a fitting end.

"Jake!" Tucker yelled, his voice loud in his head, echoing in the chamber. Nothing but the dust stirred. "Damn it, Jake," he said under his breath, acknowledging the man he had once known.

Tuc rolled to his back and gazed up in awe at the huge broken beam above him.

"Aaaarrrgh!" he yelled into the dark night, trying to release all the pain in his body and his heart.

Then he closed his eyes and wept for the only time in his adult life, for the loss of his friend and his brother.

29

There was a bang and a loud hissing sound. B jumped between the door and her human wards, barking.

"B!" Bev called her back, but the dog persisted. Whoever it was would know that there was at least a dog present.

The sound of chains and creaking wood and metal and suddenly the mine door was gone. A blast of daylight flooded the cavern entry, temporarily blinding Bev.

Sam groaned at the noise, but remained unconscious. B moved closer to him and barked at the unknown.

Bev struggled to her feet her forearm over her eyes trying to see into the light. Unsure what she was about to face, but hopeful help had miraculously come.

The first figure through the door was silhouetted in the dust. A man, military by his dress.

Relief swept over Bev, she was about to cry again and started to speak to the man when the second figure stepped into the light.

This figure was unmistakable. Long, lean, female, feline.

Bev's heart sank. She heard them speaking in familiar Spanish voices.

"Tu padre me habló del Tesoro," the man said.

"Ayudará a pagar la revolución," the woman replied.

Carlotta Corrales and her Captain, Bev thought as she backed up to Sam, positioning herself with B in front of him.

The movement and the dog caught El Capitán's attention and he stopped, shocked. He obviously didn't expect anyone to be inside the cave.

"Señorita," he said, drawing his boss' attention to the cave wall, putting his arm instinctively in front of her for protection.

Carlotta also looked surprised. An emotion Bev was sure she didn't experience much in her calculated world. In an instant her face shifted to disgust and anger. She turned on her escort.

"Cómo pasó esto? Cómo siguen vivas?" She gestured to Bev, Sam and dog.

"No se, Señorita," El Capitán chuckled in disbelief.

His mistress was not amused and turned to Bev. "You killed my father. Now you will die, if I have to do it myself." Her accent was thick and emotionless. B continued to bark viciously. "Cállate ese perro!" she screamed at the Captain. "Mátalas!"

El Capitán's smirk disappeared. Both Bev and B knew instinctively before the soldier drew his weapon what the command had meant. They both lunged at El Capitán as he drew his weapon.

The move was unexpected and they were on him, all three hitting the ground hard. The dog bit and tore at his exposed arms and face. When the man regained his breath he was screaming and bleeding. Bev struggled to hold his weapon arm.

The gunshot rung loud and repeated in the chamber, deafening them and stopping the fray on the ground. El Capitán and Bev both mentally checking the where and who of the gunshot.

Carlotta stood over Sam. Her smoking gun pointed at his temple. Sam lay silent, oblivious.

"The next one is for him," she said.

El Capitán struggled to his feet, pushing off the dog and grabbing Bev using her as a shield against B's attacks. His gun muzzle pushed hard into Bev's temple.

B turned her full attention towards the woman threatening her master. At full speed she started across the cave floor and was mid-air in her attack when Carlotta aimed and fired the gun. B's body collapsed with a yelp just before the full force of her lunge hit her intended target mid-chest, toppling the woman backwards.

Carlotta's gun clattered onto the rocky floor, her arms and legs flailed and grasped for something to grab onto as she and the lifeless dog fell backwards several steps ending suddenly as they tipped into the black abyss behind her. There was no time for her to scream as her long lean body crashed into the rocks far below.

As if in slow motion with no sound, Bev screamed for the dog and broke away from El Capitán, running for the edge of the cavern. In the back of her mind she heard his gun cock and felt his aim on her, but all she could think about was the loyal, faithful companion lost over the edge.

Time was suspended and she peered into the dark hole calling B's name, half expecting her to leap back onto the precipice.

From the shadows behind she heard a growl that at first she impossibly thought was the dog. Instead, Sam raged out of the darkness, making a furious guttural sound that was part injured animal and part human despair.

He attacked the armed soldier, slamming him against the wall and falling on top of him on the floor. El Capitán's gun fired aimlessly and when they landed his head hit the ground with sudden finality. Sam continued yelling, prostrate on top of him, making sure that El Capitán wasn't getting up, making sure the last thing El Capitán heard as he left this earth was the anguish Sam felt.

Bev collapsed in a heap. All of her energy was gone. The physical pain in her body forgotten as her heart broke.

She sobbed once again, the accumulation of all her emotions, fear, love, loss, and relief, rolled into one mournful wail. Sam crawled to where she lay, tears running down his face and falling on hers. He wrapped his body around her and they held each other and cried.

30

______

Father Juan Carlos took a deep purposed breath. He loved the smell of the church, the beeswax that coated the thick stucco walls, the lemon oil on the mesquite wood benches, the fine desert dust mixed with the scent of burned sage incense and candle wax, it was clean and cathartic. He loved the heavy silence in the cool air of the morning desert. He could hear his heart, he could hear his thoughts, and he could hear his God. He loved his God and he loved the place God had placed him to serve.

There was a connection with this place and with his service that was ordained and predestined and he didn't take it lightly. Not a day went by that the love of Father Miguel, the epitome of the love of God itself, didn't cross his mind.

It was that love that had called him to this ultimate life of service. A love that drove him and sustained him during his theological training and culminated in his ordination to the priesthood as the youngest priest of the order at 17. He knew he had much to learn about being a priest and about his God and Savior. With all gladness he wanted nothing else but to spend his life in this holy pursuit.

As much as he loved to dwell in daily prayers and supplication, today his thoughts were on his schedule. He had his first wedding to perform and did not want to be late. He instructed the acolyte at the door to light the extra candles in the windows and along the aisle.

"What a wonderful picture of God's love for his beloved church," he contemplated God's design for marriage as he crossed himself and left the sanctuary and headed to the courtyard. Juan Carlos had been overjoyed when the couple requested him personally and more than amazed at God's providence when he realized their personal connection.

The courtyard was lit with not only spring sunshine, but with the joy of love and hope for a blessed future. Brightly colored paper streamers danced from tree limbs and the fountain in the center bubbled happily. The families and towns people would gather after the ceremony and eat and dance and celebrate the couple.

The groom was not catholic and had spent several months converting to the faith, this would be he and Father Carlos' last official meeting before the wedding to complete his conversion. The groom would be baptized.

Juan Carlos spied his figure striding across the field towards the church. He was hard to miss and seemed just as stately and full of purpose as he had the first time the two had met several years ago when Juan Carlos was a child. The priest waited and as the lawman approached he could see a sincere grin on his broad face, an unmistakable look of excitement, anticipation and appreciation.

Father Carlos reached for the big man's hand and shook it with the warmth of true friendship.

"Father!" Tuc Montgomery's enthusiasm for the day came through in every action and was infectious.

Father Carlos laughed out loud, "Mr. Montgomery, your happiness is written all over your face."

Tuc grinned even wider, "I can't think of when I've been this happy."

The two men embraced.

"Bless you my brother. You deserve every happiness." The young priest was sincere. What a different world it would have been had their two paths never collided, literally.

"Thank you, son." There was a deep serious note in Tuc's voice.

Father Carlos cocked his head, "That's Father to you, sir!'

They both laughed.

"Let's do this." Tuc matter-of-factly wrapped his arm around the younger man's shoulders and turned him towards the church.

"Si, Señor," replied the priest.

31

———

Bev was excited. The kind of excitement that can only be described as childish. She didn't care. It had been such a long time since she felt like this, she wanted to just enjoy it. After all, she deserved it. So did Sam.

The past three months of physical, mental and emotional healing had been difficult. They made it through rehab and interrogation by two national, two state and one local government. Amidst all of that, they hashed out their broken hearts, both from hurting each other and from their common loss, realizing that they could help each other mend. They weren't finished dealing with it all, but they were together, they were in love, they were healing and right now they were happy.

She placed the big box with a loosely placed lid on the far side of the living room. The little Christmas tree in the corner seem to feel Bev's enthusiasm, glittering and twinkling in response. The whole room smelled of the season, fir, cinnamon and burning logs.

Sam sat contentedly by the fireplace tending the crackling fire. Firelight shown on his face and Bev took a deep breath. She sincerely loved that man. He turned and grinned as if knowing her thoughts.

"Is it time to open presents yet?" He teased.

"Just about." She crossed the room and pressed up against him, giving him a kiss.

"Well that might be the best present I've ever gotten," he quipped, leaving the fire tending and holding her tight.

There was such security there, Bev didn't ever want to be without that feeling again. She grinned through the kiss.

"You can open this present later," she promised

"Okay then," he feigned momentary disappointment then grabbed a present from under the tree and thrust it in her hands, his grey eyes twinkling. "Then open this."

Bev laughed and they sat on the floor next to the tree in front of the fire.

It was a small box, lovingly wrapped obviously by a man's hand, giving it extra charm that touched her heart. Being a girl she knew it wasn't *the* small box, but that wasn't what was on her mind at the moment anyhow. She just wanted to love him and love this moment. No future pressure, no expectation, just what was here and now.

He was almost more excited about the present than she was, so she opened it quickly. The hinged box inside the wrapped box was a red velvet jewelry box and she glanced up at him with a questioning look. He just grinned.

The little hinges creaked as she opened it and revealed a beautiful silver necklace with an unusual pendent. A rough cut stone heart of sandy rock with a bold vein of silver ore running through it, seemingly joining the two halves of the heart together.

"This isn't..?" She began to put two and two together.

"Ha!" He clapped his hands. "If you're thinking from the Silver Door Mine... then...yes."

"Oh my God!"

He scrambled to put it around her neck. "I know we discussed after we left there that the treasure was surely cursed, but I don't believe that." He touched the pendant on her chest. "That mine, that place, that life experience led us to each other...to here and now. I don't ever want to forget it. I hope you don't either."

Bev felt the tears well up. "Of course I don't ever want to forget that. I love it. I love you. And I'll wear it always. How did you get it?"

Sam looked mischievous, a sparkle in his eye. "Oh, I don't know...maybe while I was lying there in the bottom of that mine, it crossed my mind that I could die there so I kept my thoughts on living, on getting out, on you...and I stuffed a few things in my pocket."

"Wait..a few things?" Bev's insatiable curiosity was peaked.

Sam laughed, "Yeah, a few."

Bev was astounded and wanted to interrogate it out of him when a rustling from the corner reminded her of her current mission.

Sam was startled by the sound and started in its direction.

"No, no, no," Bev stopped him. "It's your turn. Go sit down," she commanded playfully. He complied.

She brought the large, obviously unbalanced box out of the corner and placed it carefully in front of him. Before he could begin to open it, the box began to move and a faint mournful whimper came from inside. Sam raised his eyebrow and looked at her just as the lid popped off and a black and tan fuzz ball pushed her way from underneath.

"Ha!" he exclaimed lifting the German shepherd pup under her front legs to see her face-to-face. Sam's eyes glistened and his voice caught. "Well, I'll be," he managed as the puppy licked his chin and wiggled with pure devotion.

"Her name is C. She's one of the narcotic unit's new trainees. They want you to be her new partner." Bev came over to be in on the love. Sam held the puppy close.

"She's the best gift I've ever gotten." He pulled Bev into the hug and whispered into her ear, "Except for you."

C barked in response, licking them both.

THE END

ABOUT THE AUTHOR

Robin Balogh Cox spent her first 50 years working as a wife and mother of three, much of it under the big skies of Texas. She has been fortunate enough to live and travel in the most beautiful places in the west and desert southwest. Places like Utah, New Mexico, Arizona, Wyoming and Colorado, as well as Texas, are a big influence in her writing. Her general love for the history, art and culture of the old west shines through in her mystery novels.

9 781943 990276